How the Little Pine
Escaped the Ax

How the Little Pine Escaped the Ax

Arthur Barnett

Library of Congress Control Number:		2010907519
ISBN:	Hardcover	978-1-4500-0891-4
	Softcover	978-1-4500-0890-7

This book was printed in the United States of America.

To order additional copies of this book, contact:
Xlibris Corporation
1-888-795-4274
www.Xlibris.com
Orders@Xlibris.com
33254

One Christmas Day, an elderly couple lived on a farm near the forest. All their children had grown up; therefore, nobody was home but the two of them. A few minutes before dinner, the wife looked around and said, "Daddy, there's something missing here." The husband replied, "What, my dear?" The wife continued, "We have been married fifty years, I don't ever remember Christmas without a tree in our home." The husband said, "You're right. You go fix dinner, and I will be right back.

The husband grabbed his ax, put it on his shoulder, and went off to the woods. He knew exactly where to find a little pine tree. As soon as he entered into the woods, the animals telegraphed a message through the woods: *Farmer in the woods on Christmas morning with an ax!*

The Little Pine Tree was so afraid. Tears ran from the Little Pine Tree. Near the Little Pine Tree were the Old Oak Trees, which God had blessed to have escaped the farmer's ax. They had grown tall in height and deep in depth. They heard the cry of the Little Pine Tree. They rose up their limbs and shaded their leaves until the Little Pine Tree was secured from the eyes of the farmer with the ax. The farmer stopped and looked and looked. He said to him, *I am sure that tree was right about here.* But his eyes could not see what the Old Oak Trees had hidden from him.

Soon he said to himself, *Maybe somebody else had beaten me to it!* So he put his ax on his shoulder and returned home, sad because he couldn't fine the Little Pine Tree. The Old Oak Trees hurried the Little Pine out of the woods into another one, gave their blessings on it that it may grow strong, tall in height, and deep in depth. So this is how the Little Pine escaped the ax.

I told you this fictional story because of a real life story I want to tell you about. It happened in my family in the 1800s. How I arrived at that figure? I subtracted 110 from 1934, and the difference is 1824. I don't know the exact year, but I know I'm close. As I go along, I will try to make it clear to you.

In the nineteenth century, there was an island twenty-six miles south of Vicksburg, Mississippi, named Jeff Davis Ben, named after the discoverer. The island was thirty square miles, divided into four sections: west, Hurricane; center, Brimfield; east Arsenal; and north, Palmyra. Arsenal was where they kept the slaves and hard-core criminals. When we were small, our father carried the boys down to see the awful place they called living quarters.

You could see the bars to the cell windows approximately one foot wide by one and a half foot high. The old wooden bunkers they had for bed had sacks filled with straw, sometimes nothing. Oh, by the way, all my eighteen brothers and sisters were born on this island. The firstborn were twins that died, but sixteen survived. Hurricane is where we lived. In the nineteenth century, one slave owner in Hurricane had so many slaves; he had to put numbers on them to keep count.

And in the spring of the year he came riding, looking over his slaves, so he stopped to speak with one of his wee hand, and his name was Manuel. Every farmer had a horse he rode called a saddle horse. The horse had a fast walk between trails; it could cover a lot a land faster than any horse walking. This day he stopped to talk to his number 1 field. After that was over, he rode off when he got to the end of the row of cotton. He heard something behind him. It was Manuel. He said to Manuel, "Don't do that anymore! It's too hard for any man to do!"

I reckon Manuel thought he cared for him! Manuel's wife and oldest daughter worked in the field. I don't know their names. The youngest was too small to work in the field. The older slaves, who were too old to work in the field, took care of the kids while the others worked. Her name was Daphne. A few days later, the same old master was riding along the same path. If you had on a number, you would have to work in that order all day, no excuses! I don't know her number, but her father was number 1. She was out of order. The master asked the young lady, "Why are you out of order?"

"I can't keep up with the man, he is too strong for me," she answered.

He said, "Wench, when I finish with you, you will be glad keeping up!" He called three slave men to hold her. They pulled her dress over her head and began to beat her.

The word reached Manuel; they have his daughter down.

Manuel picked up his hoe and came running. He killed Old Master; he killed the three slaves who held her. Manuel's luck ran out; the guards killed him, his daughter, and his wife. They went to the quarters to kill the baby! The older slaves hid her; they took chances with their own lives to hide her.

God got the news to the elders—hide the kid, the butchers are coming. They risked their own lives to save Daphne. They got her out by night to the Palmyra section to another slave master. This is where she grew up. One day the new master took notice of this young lady. She was a good worker; in my days, she worked with energy. He asked her to come to the house to babysit. The slaves called it the big house.

Now this is where the word *house nigger* came from, but this was an unusual house nigger. Somewhere or sometime, she had heard the words "Lord God Almighty." She called on him! When she called on him, he heard her and answered her prayers.

Nobody told me where Daphne learned about this name, the names *Lord God Almighty* or *Jehovah*. Perhaps she learned it from her father, Manuel, her mother, or her new family. Well, I don't think it really matters. But what really matters is that He heard her cry. He saw the tears from her eyes flow down her cheeks, and he wiped them away.

Every week the *Delta Queen*, a large pleasure boat, came down the Mississippi River. All the big slave owners would take a trip down to New Orleans. This new slave master, this week he would take his family on the trip. They took Daphne to keep their baby while they had a good time somewhere in the midst of Old Miss, the river. Most of the people in Mississippi, Louisiana, called it Old Miss.

God decided to deliver Daphne! God called the clouds from the west, the thunder from the south, the lighting from the north, and the wind from the east. They all came together in the midst of Old Miss. Old Miss got trouble. The waves rocked the *Delta Queen* until she was almost ready to go down.

Daphne, with the baby, ran out on deck of the boat and fell down on her knees. With the little white baby in her arms, she called out the name that she had learned from somebody: Jehovah. Her prayer was, "Don't cut me off from the face of the earth! They killed my father, my mother, and my sister, please don't cut me off."

Soon the wind stopped, the waves stood still, and the boat straightened up. When they got to the first stop, the slave owner's wife walked up to Daphne, asked for her baby, and said, "You are a free slave, Daphne."

Daphne continued to grow strong and later became Daphne Riggs. She died when I was twelve years old. Daphne was a 110 years old, and she was my great-grandmother.

The Little Pine Tree is dead now; her roots spring up a thousand or more miles across America. I'm Arthur Barnett.

Daphne is free now! No place to lay her head, no food to eat, only the garment on her back. A family took her in. I don't know the family name, and they lived on the Stewart plantation. One day she was working in the field, and she was noticed by Stewart. He asked her to come and work in the "big house." That's what the slaves called it—the big house. This time she was recognized for a different reason. Dathney was an attractive young lady, and she did her work well with a lot of energy.

In those days, they would have her come to work there so that they could have a white wife to carry out Saturday night and a black mistress throughout the week to take care of the kids. At night, Old Boss Stewart's wife noticed he was coming to bed a little late. She didn't say anything to him when she caught him coming from Dathney's shack out back. She told him she had to leave at once, but he didn't want her to leave. His wife said, "If you don't, I will tell all your friends you are going to bed with a black woman, an ex-slave at that."

So he had to let Dathney go, but the damage had been done. Daphne had given birth to her first son, Jim Stewart. She named her son Jim Stewart after his father. She went to the Scott plantation where she met her husband Manuel Riggs, an escaped slave from Texas. Louisiana slaves were free a year before Texas, and they got married there. Their firstborn was Martha Riggs; we called her Big Sis. Then there were Elli Riggs, Pete Riggs, Jane Riggs, Amelia Riggs (my grandmother), William Riggs, Mary Riggs, and Arthur Riggs (everybody called him Bus Riggs). They all grew up in the same plantation. Elli grew up a little too fast. He swung on the old man and knocked him to his knees. Daphne went to run in between them, but the old man stood back and said, "Honey, this thing has to be settled today! Who will be the man of the house, my son or me?" And in a split second Ellac was out cold. The old man was the head of the house, and he proved it. So Ellac had to leave at once; no longer could he live under the same roof.

I didn't know Elli until he was well up in age. He was a well-developed man and could pick up three to four hundred pounds of cotton a day. So the rest took good advice from Ellac: don't try Dad. Soon they all grew and got married. Pete married Hattie, Bus married Ollie, Martha married a fellow called Big Bud, and Mary married Willie Green. In her late years, Amelia went to work for a rich family named Barnett, first as a maid and later as a mistress. I will tell you all about it later. I'm trying to keep everything in its time frame.

At Scott plantation trouble came. Scott held a gun on one of Bus and Pete's friends and beat him with an axe handle. The word got to Bus and Pete. They ran Scott in his house, and he didn't come out for a week. They threatened to beat his hind parts the way he beat their friend.

Of course, you knew they had to move. They came twenty-six miles north of Newton, Louisiana into Madison Parish, where they met Ed Adams. He was happy to see them, and they reached an agreement. Adams built homes and barns for the stock in a place named Trinidad. It was a place just suitable for the Riggs to make a good living. When they moved, they brought all their friends with them, but Amelia Riggs stayed in Tensas Parish living with the Barnetts. Soon there came two little red boys, one named Jim Barnett and another named Willie Barnett. The Barnett family decided to kill her over the two boys, and Barnett went over the river to Davis Ben. He bought a place called Hurricane, and they built homes eighteen feet off the ground. Every year, Old Miss would flood the island, which was thirty square miles.

The island had everything you needed to make a good living. Barnett sent his son Jim to Vicksburg Catholic School; they couldn't deny him the privilege because his dad was rich and Catholic. One son went to school to get an education, and the youngest one stayed home to educate himself on how to make corn liquor. All the rich people said he made the best corn liquor in the world. When he died in 1977, my sisters said there were more rich white people than family crying at his funeral. Willie was one of a kind; if God had to make another Willie Barnett, I'm sure he would use the same frame. I don't know a whole lot about him; mostly my knowledge about him was told by my mother, but what I saw was enough. I wanted him to be like my father, but he was Willie Barnett, not Jim Barnett, so I missed out a lot. Not being reared on the island like my sisters and brothers, I didn't know him as "Bro Willie." I called him "Uncle Willie."

He may have invented the pants boys wear today, down on his hips, shirttail out with a half pint in his hind pocket. Every ten or fifteen minutes he would stop and get himself a drink. He didn't bother anybody, and if you had good sense you wouldn't bother him, white or black. Willie died early. My dad had to come out of that all-white school in Vicksburg. Barnett's secretary knew all about the business and took over. Amelia remarried a few years later to James

Roan. Later, they had four daughters and a son. The girls had their school on the island, and his son was the youngest and went to school in Chicago or San Francisco. He was pretty well educated, and so were the girls. Three took complexion after him, one after her. They were all beautiful ladies: Apple Tina, Mary Lou, Ophelia, and Constena. Roann was a smart fellow; he knew how to make a dollar. He and Willie teamed up, and he said, "Willie, you make the booze and I'll make the contact."

He made a deal with the *Delta Queen* and sold booze in the middle of the Mississippi River. I was over there once, and they took me out with them. I saw men carrying five-gallon cases on their shoulders and leaving them on the boat. When the *Delta Queen* got close, they blew the horn, which meant to get ready to hook up. Once a week, the *Delta Queen* would go to New Orleans to have a good time. They had an eighteen-foot barge and a small boat, the only transportation on the island, so the Feds couldn't get over there. The island was rich with everything—pecans, wild game, wild hogs, deer; and the rich bankers would come down from Vicksburg to spend the weekend.

According to James Wade (everybody called him Manson), a good guitar player, my dad also played, and Willie, when he was sober, blew the sax. From Friday evening till Sunday evening, my grandmother's stove fire never went out cooking and frying fish, and we would be drinking booze. Roann was handling all the money. In the fall on the year, the Riggs would come over and bring their friends to make a few dollars picking up pecans. They would go out in the morning. By twelve o'clock, they could have a barrel, and Roann would buy them. At night, they got drunk and danced all night, and Roann got his money right back. He was a shrewd fellow. I don't think he drank. Willie peeped the rich guy's hole card. Oh, one would think old Willie was a drunk, and he didn't know what's going on. Wicked men came down to taunt old Willie's sisters. Willie grabbed his shotgun, started shooting, and those bankers ran in one of those lakes close to the house.

Grandmother jumped in front of the banker to keep Willie from shooting him, and he fired on her. Manson said he ran and left his guitar. He said he was running so fast, but he heard something behind him; and when he looked around, the chickens were running too, getting away from Willie. I was told he would give you the shirt off his back, but if you made him mad, he would take your shirt off your back. My dad peeped Roann's hole card and told his mother that Roann was a crook, but she didn't believe him. By this time, Jim was grown, and he had met a young lady right close to where they would land their boats on Louisiana side, in a place called Somerset. Her name was Rosie Reddman. They got married, and he carried her over the river on the island and built a home eighteen feet off the ground because every year the Old Miss would flood the island.

Soon the babies started coming: a set of twins that died, Irene Barnett (Son Barnett, that's what everyone called him), Aldene Barnett, Lillie Barnet, James Barnett (we call him Man), Philip Barnett, the one and only Arthur Barnett (they call me Pudding), Carolyn Barnett (we call her Cat), Virginia Barnett (we call her Gennie, after grandmother Gennie Reddman), Hubbert Barnett (Hub), and Leon Barnett. I think I'm right about the younger one. Next was Ernest Barnett. They stopped for ten years and later they caught their second wind; and they started back Dalnetia Barnett, Barbara Barnett, and Earl Barnett. These are my brothers and sisters with Jim and Rosie Barnett.

My father kept telling his mother that Roann was robbing her blind of all the money he was making and sending to a Los Angeles bank. One day she went to the bank for a little change, and she didn't have a cent. "The Riggs" rose up in that woman, and she went back and drew her gun on him. "You half-white SOB," she said, "I should blow your damn brains out of your damn head." She beat him and took him to the train station to get a ticket to Los Angeles.

"You half-white SOB, if you ever put your feet back anywhere in Louisiana, I will hunt you down and kill you."

Roann must have believed her because he never came back. He had a lien on the plantation at Vicksburg Bank. Boy, he really robbed my family.

Now I believe it was 1922 when the Riggs left Tensas and came to Trinidad. Trinidad was nothing but wilderness, and the Riggs and their friends cleared that land, planted cotton and corn, and made money. Ed Adams said they made enough money they could have owned Tallulah. Old man Riggs had died, so they brought Dathney, their mother, with them. Dathney lived with Jane in an old slave owner's house. It was so big they had two fireplaces, a large hall, an acre yard fenced in, and fifty acres of clear grass for their horses and cows.

The Riggs didn't have any children to help them with the farm. Uncle Pete had one son, and Aunt Martha also had one son; his name was Sarge Gibson. So they would go over on the island and begged on my dad. Aunt Mary asked to let Pap come stay with her for a little while, so Dad agreed and she brought him to Trinidad. Now Bus thought they would try their luck. Bus said, "Let me take Pudding so he can play with his brother, and the next time we come over, we will bring him back." After six months and still no Pudding, my mother said, "Jim, go get my son." The Riggs went to their sister to talk to my dad—to let them help him out, let them keep me and my brother.

My mother agreed to let them keep Pap, but not me. The Riggs talked to my grandmother. She got my dad, and they finally wore my mother down. She never agreed. I was one year old when Bus and Ollie got me. They didn't have a babysitter, so they would take me to the field and make me sit under a large tree. One summer day, when they were picking cotton, they put me on a quilt and let me sit under a tree with a slice of watermelon. For some reason I crawled out from under the tree to the old dusty road. Adams came along looking over his farm and ran over me. My mother heard me cry. She said, "That man has run over my child." She got out and ran the old Model T Ford down. He saw her coming holding up her hand, and he stopped. Ollie was almost out of breath. She said, "Man, you have run over my child." Adams said, "What child? I haven't seen any child." He came back, put her and me into the car, and went to town. They went to a doctor. My hip was broken, and my skull was cracked. Adams told the doctor, "If you can't do him any good, I will run him over to Vicksburg." The doctor said, "I can fix him up, and he will never know that his hip was broken, he will be OK."

I stayed at Adams' home six long months with a private nurse. After six months in Adams's home, he wanted to adopt me. Ollie said, "Under no circumstances will I give up my son." My own mother couldn't have loved me any more than Ollie. She stood between me and a lot of abuse I may have had as a child. Bus was a mean uncle. Mom stood between me and him; she wasn't afraid of him. He was mean to me. I saw him cock his pistol in her face. She just sat there, and I was sitting beside her.

Now I was better, up running around. Too small to work in the fields and no more shade trees. At the big house where Dathney and grandmother lived was where I stayed during those days. Dathney was too old to work. She was over a hundred years old then. Stella Riggs was in charge. She was the eldest of William Riggs's daughters. Her sister Jane didn't have any kids. Every day at twelve o'clock, Dathney would call us; we would sit down around her, and she would tell us about her troubles and how she came up.

I must admit I wasn't a bad boy but did a few nasty things. I remember one Sunday morning, Mom had fixed breakfast—fried chicken, rolls, grits, and eggs. Mother called, "Son, breakfast ready."

I went to the table, looked, and said, "I don't want this."

Bus jumped up, grabbed me by the collar. "You little bastard," he said, "you're not going to eat this food."

Mother jumped up between him and me and said, "Keep your hands off my son."

"You're ruining that damn boy."

"If I ruin him, let me ruin him. He's my son."

A mother's love for her sons, now I see that in my marriage. I won't go there now; I have a lifetime to go, I hope.

"Son, what do you want?"

"Some syrup and biscuits and a glass of milk. I didn't like chicken, and I didn't eat chicken." She fixed the biscuits for me; that was my breakfast.

Dathney strapped my hind part one day. She was afraid of anything that looked like a gun. I had a cap pistol that I was shooting, and she asked me to stop. When she turned around, I fired it right behind her. She jumped and said whoopee, and I took off. Dathney said, "Catch that little dirty rascal." And soon Stella Riggs caught me. Dathney put a whipping on my hind part I will never forget.

In 1927, a flood came and water got in our house from the Old Mississippi River. When everything got back to normal that fall, after crop harvest was over, School Time Country School opened the first week in October.

Country school had six months. The teacher had to teach you in six months what the city school taught in nine months. The country teacher had her work cut out for her, and she had your work for you too! Our first school was a mile from home, and our teacher's name was Ms. Chaffers. She was about forty years old. The people in these days said if you got old and hadn't been married, then something was wrong with you. They didn't say what was wrong with her, but they said *something* was wrong! But she was our first teacher, and you'll never guess who was the teacher's pet—Old Pudding. She brought me apples every day. I sat up with her and not with the other kids. The other kids are getting their lesson and I'm eating apples. So Bus said, "Get him out and close the school down." Ms. Chaffers didn't come back the next fall.

Now we have three miles instead of one to walk. Some mornings that winter, wind would be right in our faces. Stella Riggs, Voila Page, Aunt Hattie's granddaughter, and Uncle Pete's wife, walked to school together. Right where they closed the first school there was a big curve in the road. There would be a busload of white kids waiting to kick our hind part. Every morning and evening, they would be there, standing on the outside and saying, "Come on, nigger, we going to kick your ass." Mother would fix me a good lunch in my bucket; she would have two hot baked sweet potatoes. I would wrap them up and put them in my pockets to keep my hands warm.

Before I get where the fight started, I would eat all I could, throw the rest out, and fill the bucket with rocks to fight with. They would be hollering, "We're gonna kick the hell out of you." And we would reply, "Yes, we are going to kick the hell out of your white ass too!" As Stella and Voila led the way, Pap, my brother, opened our bucket full of choice rocks for our slingshot. Stella Riggs was fighting like a black panther. I saw she had two white girls, one under each arm and kicking the hell out of another. Voila was swinging her lunch bucket full of rocks. By the time, the fight was going for or against Saul McSimpson, West McSimpson, James Gibson, and Cursena Cambell (later became Cursena Riggs). We knew all those kids, and they knew us. The fight would go on for about five or ten minutes, and they would get back on the bus. I had my slingshot drawn on Verior Buford; but before I turned it loose, she cried, "Pudding, don't you shoot me with that nigger shooter." So I didn't.

They got back on the bus and said, "Nigger, we'll be waiting on your black ass this evening." And we replied, "And we'll be looking for your white ass." Now we have two more miles to go. Some days we would run a little late, all the kids sitting around the red-hot old potbellied stove. Mrs. Gertrude would make them get back so we could get warm. Every evening, just like clockwork, sometimes they would pass us on the way, hollering, "Hurry up an' come on, nigger, we're going to whip the hell out of you this evening." The eight of us would put our books down and go at it. I'm going to go back a little. When dinner came at the school, I wouldn't have anything to eat but two sweet potatoes. The kids started joking me, calling me sweet potato pudding. All I didn't eat up that morning I would dump out, Pap and I.

Soon we got a little help from the boys from the school. Of course, you know our school was also our church. The boys from school would go ahead of us and hide in the ditch. They got out of the bus, girls fighting girls and boys fighting boys. When we got there they jumped out of the bus, and the eight of us dropped our books ready to fight. The eight big boys were on the blind side of the bus, and when everybody got out of the bus but the driver (his name was Lloyd Piper and he was eighteen), those black boys came out of the ditch. Two went on the bus and closed the door, and they worked Lloyd's hind part over. Someone hollered, "Look at them damn niggers, where do they come from?" We beat them so good they couldn't get back on the bus. Someone said that Pap and Pudding were shooting those damn nigger shooters; they might have said something because we were the only ones shooting. I was good at it. I broke all the glass out of the bus, and they had twelve miles to go to town to school. Soon they took Lloyd off the bus and put an elder fellow on it. His name was Alfonzo. They would wave at us and shake their fist, and we would pat our behind at them.

I'm going to go back a few days. Remember the white young lady who said "Pudding, don't you shoot me with that nigger shooter"? Well, they had a large orchard. We used to go down there, and her mother would let us go in there and eat all the fruit we could eat. When we came out, we would play house with the three girls—Wyree Buford, the older one; Verior Buford (later in the years, she won the Louisiana beauty contest); and the youngest one we called Little Sister (I didn't know her real name). The Collins and Alfonzo all had big families, and we didn't have any trouble out of these people. They were fine people. Lloyd Piper was older and put those kids up to fight us, but he got his hind part beaten up to pay for it. We never did tell our family what was happening. We looked forward to every morning to fight. In the mid-'30s, there was a group of treasure hunters going throughout the south hunting for treasure. Soon they found their way to Trinidad. The big house where Dathney lived was a slave owner's house. The one-acre yard with two large wells was bricked in, one on the east end of the house and one on the west end. Three huge oak trees in front of the house looked to be a hundred years old.

When the south found out they were losing the war, they buried their money—all gold. Some had barrels of money. They would give a slave a shovel, and the slave would dig the hole. Old Master would ask him to swear that he would guard this money with his life. And the slave would say, "Yassir." I imagine what the slave was thinking, *As soon as you gone I will steal it an' buy my freedom.* Old Boss was thinking otherwise, *When he swore, I would kill him and bury him with the money so that if anybody tried to dig up his money, his spirit would scare them away.* Whatever you were afraid of, if you were trying to dig up the money, his spirit would appear in that form. If you were afraid of snakes, his spirit would appear in the form so you would run.

One day, two white fellows showed up from Chicago with a treasure-finding machine. They contacted Bus and Pete, and they gave the OK to try it out. So between the well and the house was a hidden treasure. Bus and Pete gave him permission to dig, and Bus, Pete, Steve, Kincy, and Anthony Reed did the digging. The deal was they would share fifty-fifty, and the next night they dug. Mother said, "Son, let us go up to see what's going on," so we went, and they were digging with shovels. The headman, the fellow to tame the spirits, sprinkled sulfur around the hole and burned it so that the spirits couldn't cross over. He went about ten yards away from the hole, and he had the Bible in his hand. My mother lifted me up to the window so I could see. She said he was reading the Bible backwards, and he was gonna burst hell wide open. They dug until they came to a brick wall, and they started to break through the wall. Andy Reed said you could hear the money on the other side. The man in charge told them to stop because he couldn't handle the spirit any longer. So they all went home tired and went to sleep, and the crook came back and stole the money. The next morning they got their cars and guns, but it was too late—they were long gone.

On the west side of the house was another well, but every time they tried to dig it up, water would come and cover the hole. So they gave up. Bus, WW, one was a drawing for $12 a month—big money in those days. Farm was making pretty good money. He and my mother were well dressed and owned a pretty good car. He and Pete lived on the same plantation owned by Saunders. A large family lived on it. Jones was their name. Simon Jones had five or six daughters, all very fair-looking ladies. Bus and Pete were going out with two sisters, Bus with Jerdene and Pete with Bay Bay. Bus bought his woman a suit that cost $40 and bought my mother one just like it. One Sunday, they both showed up at church dressed alike. Monday morning at the breakfast table, Mother asked Bus, "Why did you buy mine the same color?" Bus just got choked at the table. Bus and one of the men in the Jones family had a run-in. His name was

Addlee. Addlee had the upper hand because he had a knife, and his family was behind him. Bus had to back down, but he promised Addlee, "If you ever cross me again, I will kill you."

Addlee was reared up in Saunders home with his own son. From what I was told, he reared Addlee from three years old. I didn't hear anything about Saunders being Addlee's dad. In those days, a lot of white farmers had babies by some of the black women on these farms. In 1929 Bus took sick, bad off sick. He went to every doctor in town. He went to Mississippi, and they couldn't do him any good. Something was choking him to death. When he had those attacks, you could hear him gasping for breath. One day he had one, and his brothers and sisters thought that he was dead. Soon I looked up the old dusty road, and you would never guess who I saw coming—Dathney Riggs with a dress down to her ankles, which was the way she wore all her dresses. At 105 years old, she was walking faster than I do now. She pulled her dress up a little, came to the house, and went straight to bed. She pulled his eyes open and said, "Thank God, he ain't dead yet." She turned to my mother and asked, "Do you have any red pepper?" Mother said yes and told me to go to the garden and get my grandmother some pepper. I ran to the garden and got three red peppers. Dathney said, "Make a fire and put the pepper in some water, put it on the fire, and let it boil." Dathney said, "Bring it to me," so I did, and then she told me to take it to my mother. She said, "I know it's nasty, but let him drink as much as he can." He took two swallows, and Dathney said that was enough. Bus soon fell asleep, and Dathney went back home.

The next morning Bus woke up feeling pretty good. He ate a little something. The next morning mother and I were eating when Bus called Ollie to bring me the night pot. Mother said, "Son, take to your uncle the pot." I ran in and ran right back out because I didn't want to see someone throwing up. A few minutes later Bus called, "Ollie, Ollie."

"What is it Bus?"

"Come here quick."

She jumped up, partly running. Bus said, "Look here." In his hand was a foot, which looked like a lizard foot caught in his teeth. Mother said, "No wonder those doctor's couldn't cure you, you've been poisoned with witchcraft. God let that feet get caught in your teeth so you could see what was killing you." A few days later, Bus was up and going. He went right back where he got the poison from. His woman, he made her my godmother. Pete's woman was my brother Pap's godmother. They had a thing together.

One Saturday night, Bus, Large (his sister's son), and Pete's son (married to one of the Jones girls) were invited to a party. Bus rode his horse, and Large and Riggs both rode with him. James Wade, better known as Manson, had a little three-piece band, so they played music for the party. One of the in-laws got a little tipsy and swung on Riggs. Soon Riggs had punched Jess White out. I want to tell you a little about the Riggs family. If you jumped on them and couldn't fight, you just got your hind part whipped, man or woman. Addlee didn't like what happened to his brother-in-law, so he put on a pair of brass knuckles. Riggs told Addlee, "If you put those brass knuckles down, I will put the same thing on your hind part. While they were getting ready to double bank Riggs, Large slipped out the back and went to were Bus was. Bus was down to his woman's house lying across the bed. Large said, "Bus, you better come up here, they want to double bank Riggs." Bus got up and went to the party. He said, "You asked us up here, now you want to beat up my brother's son." Bus told them to come on. He told them to go out before him. Addlee said to Bus, "I will put a whipping on your ass." He swung at Bus, but Bus ducked out of the way. Addlee swung at him with such force he turned all the way around. That was his last turn because Bus pulled out a .32-20, pulled the trigger, and Addlee fell dead at Bus's feet. The coroner said he had never seen a shot so perfect. He hit him in the black part of his eye and didn't touch the white part. Bus and his two nephews rode away.

According to my stepbrother, at the sound of that gun, some of the family ran into the Old Mississippi. Sometimes, when you make a remark, especially a harsh one, you better be very careful because the devil will try to make you live up to it. *If you ever cross me, I will kill you.* Bus kept his promise. Twenty years later, I made that same remark, but God was on my side. I will tell you about that a little later. Now all hell had broken loose and mother and I were caught in the middle. Simon Jones was second in charge, and he rang the bell to wake up Mr. Saunders. They told him Bus had killed Addlee, and according to the report, Saunders cried like a baby. When he stopped crying he sent for the black-man hater, Sheriff Stant Bettis. Saunders got all his black people and gave them guns. Large Gibson came to the house around two thirty and called, "Ollie!" Mother said, "What is it?" Large said Bus had killed Addlee. By that time, she had lit the lamp, and she asked, "Where is he?" Large said he was sitting out in the cotton field, and I could see her almost sink to the floor. Mother asked me, "Son, did you hear that?" And I said, "Yes, I did." Soon she said, "Look, son," and I came to the door. Approximately eight carloads of black people were with Saunders and Stant Bettis. They went all around our house with their bright lights on—Stant Bettis, Mr. Saunders, his son, and one black man named Jess.

Bettis knocked at the door, and Mother went to the door and opened it. Bettis said, "Good morning, Ollie." Mother said, "Good morning, Mr. Bettis, Mr. Saunders, and your son." And they all spoke. Bettis asked, "Do you know why we're here?"

"Yassir."

"Who told you?"

"Large Gibson."

Bettis asked, "Have he been home?"

"No, sir."

Then Bettis said, "We have to search the home." And mother started to hand him the lamp. Bettis said, "You show us through."

When he walked across the door, he had his hand on the trigger. I was sitting up in bed, and when he saw me, he pointed his gun at me. Bettis asked, "Who is that?" And mother said, "My son." They went in the kitchen, the next bedroom, and the guestroom. Bettis said, "I've never been in a room fixed up so nice before." He stopped talking about Bus. He asked Mother, "Where did you get your furniture from?" Mother said, "I got it from Vicksburg." Jess, the black fellow, was looking all under the bed. They ran him out, and he made a great mistake when he went under the house. That black dog hung onto his hind part; I heard him yelling. Mother told me to get that dog off that man. I was a little slow moving, so she yelled, "Boy, get that dog." So I went under the house and made our dog, Black Boy, turn him loose. I showed them he was a little nervous, so they all got in their cars and left.

Friday evening before Bus got in trouble, Uncle Pete and Aunt Hattie ran down the road to a place in Ivory. That's where my grandmother lived, and she was on her deathbed. Someone told Bettis where Uncle Pete was, and he went down there and cocked his gun on him. Bettis said, "You black SOB, I ought to blow your damn brains out." Pete fell down on his knees with his hands up and said, "What have I done that make you want to kill me?" Bettis said, "You helped your brother get away."

"My brother got away, what had he done?" Simon Jones spoke and told Mr. Saunders to stop Bettis, that Pete didn't know what happened. Saunders told Bettis to stop, but that dirty bastard went in my grandmother's house in her bedroom and pulled the covers off her with his gun cocked. Soon they left and Uncle Pete and Aunt Hattie came home. Early Monday morning, here came Ed Adams. Boy, was the fellow angry. He came straight to Mother and said, "Ollie, tell me what happened." And mother told him word for word.

These were Adams's words, "That low-down SOB know better than to come down to my property disturbing my people without permission from me. Saunders, I will sue him, and Bettis, I will have him thrown off the force." He went to Saunders, and Saunders had to beg his pardon. It wasn't long before Bettis was gone. Saunders made a remark, "When we catch the SOB, I will have him hung. I have seven barrels of money, and I will have him hung if it takes every nickel!" Adams said, "I will make you spend every damn nickel if you want him." Adams came back the next day and told Mother, "If you know where Bus is, tell him to come home, and he won't spend one night in jail." Mother sent the word and Bus said, "Hell no! I can't take that chance." Bus said that if they caught up with him that night, he was going to shoot it out. He was going to make sure that he killed Bettis, Saunders, and his son and as many of the black asses as he could. For one year our house was watched day and night, and Mother used to say, "Son, come home before dark because I don't want them to make a mistake and shoot you. You could hear them running trying to get out of the way of Black Boy. That was one hell of a dog.

In 1934, Ford came out with a new car that could run up to ninety miles per hour, and Adams's son, little Adams bought one and sent it back to the factory and told them to put one hundred miles on it. So they did and sent it back to him. Soon he killed himself. Running too fast, the car's speedometer broke at ninety miles an hour; and when they found him, his radio was playing, "I'll be glad when you're dead, you rascal you!"

The old man Adams died shortly after. He loved that boy so. His youngest was away in law school. I will tell you about him later. The Jones family and the Riggs family went to the same church. The Joneses had the upper hand. Boss Man was dead. Sometimes you could feel the tension in church. They were smiling. "Oh, we going to have him hung because Mr. Saunders say so." The Riggs didn't say a word. Bus was over on Jeff Davis Ben, where his sister and father were. My dad had the only transportation crossing the island, and somebody told Bettis that Bus was over on the island. When they were asking questions about Bus being over there, a white plantation owner who was a friend of my dad got word to him. The law wanted to come over and get Bus from over there, but my brother put Bus on the Mississippi side of the river, and he walked to Vicksburg, to my aunt's house. Ophelia Roann was her name. All hell was fixing to break loose again. One day, one of the Riggs sisters was working our mule. They didn't ask mother anything. When Bus was there, that was the way they did things. But Bus was no longer there so you have to deal with Ollie. Ollie said, "I don't mind you using my mule, but ask me first, which was only right." You would think that mother had thrown an all-night piss pot in their faces. They did everything they could do against us. They tried to get me from Ollie. Jim said she had him ever since he was a baby. Now she needed him.

Mother had gone to Mr. Adams before he died and told him what they were trying to do. Adams said, "Let them try, I will have them to pay you $20 a day for every day you had him." So mother didn't have anything to worry about. Jane, Martha, Mary, and my grandmother told my dad that I didn't want to have anything to do with my brothers and sisters. That was a lie. When they came from over the river on Saturday, they came to Tallulah. I wanted to show my pretty sisters, and I had some pretty ones. All the boys thought I was a Riggs because I was reared by the Riggs. They saw they couldn't get me from her so they turned on me. They ran after me like I was something good to eat. One day I was over to James' house to see Stella Jane make home brew. Stella and I were playing, and she pushed me over. I fell against the churn and knocked it over. Stella ran out the back door to tell what happened, and I went out the front. James told Stella to catch me. Stella could run just like she could fight. Soon Stella was closing in on me, and I stopped to pick up a large piece of dust. Stella said, "Don't hit me I'm your cousin," trying to get close to me. I draw back, and she backed up. Soon I called that black dog. My mother said he was lying on the porch, and I saw him jump up and run and jump over the fence. My mother said to herself, "Who is at my son, he's calling for help?"

Soon I saw him coming, and so did Stella. Boy, don't you sic that dog on your cousin. She turned around, and the dog caught her. She was screaming and hollering. He didn't bite her, just pulled half of her dress. All hell broke loose. Here came Jane, Martha, and Mary. Jane said, "Where is he? I'm going to tear his hind part up." She started through the gate, and Ollie said, "Don't come through that gate. The first one to come through, I will kill." Mother stood there with a hoe. I stood on the porch with my dog. Jane said, "I will get you, little bastard." If we got a little behind on the farm, we couldn't hire any of them. We had to get some of the other farmers to help us. You couldn't outwork the women or the men. The women could chop cotton, plow, pick cotton, cut wood, sew—they could do it all. Work in the field until eleven o'clock, go home and cook dinner, and by one o'clock be ready to go back to the field. They couldn't keep a husband. They got a man, worked him till pay time, and made him run away so they could put all the money in their pocket. If you were smart you would go; if not, the brothers would see that you go.

One day those crooked women are going to meet their match, my mother would say. And just as she said that, Jane did meet her match in the form of a big six-footer, 285-pound hard worker. He was a good ball player and used to play with the Chicago Black Socks, a professional all-black team. Close to the payoff of the cotton crop as usual, Jane got messy. All of us little boys loved him, and we called him Big Chief. One day he hit Jane, knocked her down, and grabbed a double-bladed ax to hit her with. A young kid who had just moved into our farm saved her life when he grabbed hold of the ax. Chief was so strong he carried Jack around with his swing, but that gave Jane enough time to get up and run. I will tell you a little later who Big Chief was. The news got to Pete. Pete had a pet horse named Bennie, whom he saddled and went hunting with, armed with a .30-30 high-powered rifle. Pete told Chief, "I heard what you did to my sister, and I came over here to kill you, but the kids love you, so I'm afraid they will hate me if I did. Pete told Chief to get on Bennie, ride him as far as he wished. "When you get off, tie the reins up on the saddle, and Bennie will come back home." Chief did as he was told, and Bennie came back home. Now the young fellow grabbed the ax; Joe Paige was his name. Their grandmother reared him and his brother Stanley Paige, whom we called Blue. Aunt Leathie, my grandmother's sister and my great-aunt, had lost her husband in Somerset. So Pete and the two boys moved with her to Trinidad. Pete was married to Hattie Riggs.

Soon we got our own school, a new church—Mount Pilgrim Baptist Church. Our first teacher, Ms. Jordon, was a fine and elegant lady. She taught day school and taught the elders at night. I have in my possession now, my mother's certificate from fourth grade. For two years she taught, and next came the professor's daughter from uptown. I won't name her. I guess her age was twenty. She was very good-looking. Those big boys had a good time with that young lady. She lived near the church with Ms. Laura and Steve Kincy, and her father picked her up on the weekends. Mrs. Kincy, who stuttered a little when she talked, said, "Th-th-that woman got to go. I hear young men knocking all night long."

Pete said, "No, she can't come back," so she didn't. The very next year here came this movie star Myrtle Reed, classy all the way. I will come back to her. I have to back up a few years—to 1934. In the spring of 1934, Dathney lay in her deathbed. She was 110 years old. The first part of the night, at first dark, Mother and I went to see her. At approximately nine thirty, we went home, and Mother said to me, "Son, your grandmother will be dead before day. I often think about what she said. How could she be so sure she would be dead by day?

Around two thirty the same night, I heard the church bell toll. Mother woke me up and said, "Son, put on your clothes and let me see what I can do to help." This is the mother of sisters Martha, Jane, and Mary. We got our old lantern for light, and we went to the house. They were crying. Hattie came, then Pete's wife. They gave her a bath and dressed her in white. The next morning, they sent to town to get a casket and took her to church. They contacted two powerful black preachers: J. B. Campbell, who was well educated, and Lynn Henderson, who was self-educated in God's word. Campbell tried to close the door on Lynn. Campbell broke it down into how many years she had lived, how many months, weeks, days, hours, and minutes. The church was full of people, and they were stunned at the knowledge of this black preacher. When he sat down, the church stood up and applauded. He tried to close the door on Lynn, but Lynn got his foot on the door and kicked it down. The church forgot it was a funeral; they rose to their feet and cheered. You would have thought that it was a regular Sunday service. Soon they laid her casket on the back of a wagon, carried her to the burial ground, and put six feet of dirt on her face.

The old master couldn't hold her as a slave any longer
God said let her go
The grave couldn't hold her soul
It went back to God
Nor could the grave hold her blood
Her blood across America from shore to shore
More than a thousand strong and growing

(This is the end of the chapter of the *Little Pine Tree That Escaped the Ax*)

In the '30s, the Depression looked like it was a curse on the land. There was no rain sometimes. Sickness killed the farmers and hogs. After that, TB killed the cows, next the horses and mules. We had eighteen heads of hogs, six cows, and five horses and didn't lose a single animal. The Riggs lost every hog they had. Pete lost their last cow. Aunt Hattie said God wasn't fair, for He took her last cow and we still had five. I told Mother I would give them a new start with hogs. I ain't giving away one cow.

Now let's talk about Mrytle Reed, our new teacher. When we saw her coming, we put on our best behavior. We lined up boys on one side, girls on the other. When she stepped out of the car, we all said good morning aloud. She smiled back and said, "Good morning to all of you." Boy, she was as tough as she was good-looking. After she got her students lined up, some of the kids said they wished they had never seen her. In country school, one teacher taught from the first grade to the sixth. To go the seventh grade, you had to go uptown. She had to teach you in six months what the kids in town learned in nine months. When you left country school, you had to pass a test, like you do when you go to college, and not one student failed the test. When I first started in fourth grade, I went home with six books in the evening, did my little chores, ate, and sat down by the lamplight or firelight.

One day, a snowstorm came. The snow on the ground was knee-deep. I got up that morning, fed my horses and hogs, and milked one cow; and when I finished, breakfast was ready. I hurried and ate breakfast, thinking I was going to make myself a bird trap to catch some of those big black birds in my barn. My mother looked out the door and saw smoke coming out the chimney at the church. She said, "Son, put your boots on, wrap up good, and go to school."

"What do you mean, put on your clothes and go to school?" I said.

She said, "That woman came twelve miles in that snow to teach you."

"Ain't nobody going to be there but her."

"That's why I'm sending you to keep her company."

I was only fourteen, and I told my mother to get rid of all the hired help, including her son and family. "Get rid of them! I will run the farm. I was doing most of the work anyway."

The son of the helper was a guitar player, and all he wanted to do was play music, so she did what I asked. I was in luck, soon her father found an old friend whom he had known for a long time, and he came to stay with us. He was a lot of help to me, and he was company for Mother while I was away.

I couldn't get to school very much. In class, your position was determined by your grade 6 attendance. I was number 4 when I arrived at school that morning. I spoke and she said, "Good morning, I'm glad to see you, come sit close by the fire." So I sat there for approximately fifteen minutes, and she called my reading class. I went through it A-OK. Next was math. I was number 4, so I worked every fourth problem because that night, I thought the others would be there. Nobody showed up but me. Seven pages of math, and I worked every fourth one. She kept me at the blackboard for eight hours. She said, "Young man, every one of those problems are yours to work." That broke me up. I was glad that only she and I were the only ones there because those kids would have never let me forget it. You will never guess what a fifteen-year-old boy thinks when he is around a pretty twenty-year-old lady.

The big boys—Jack, Saul, West, and James—said to me one day, "I notice every time her ride is late she always ask you to stay back till her ride comes. Boy, I believe she likes you. The next time she asks you to stay back, man, I'll ask her."

I said, "Yeah, I've been sizing her up. I believe she is ready picking."

Two days later, her ride was late and she asked me to stay. *Me*, I thought, *this is my chance.*

The old potbellied stove was still hot. I was sitting close to it with my legs wide open; things began to rise. I made up my mind. *It's time to make my move.* I got up and started toward her.

She looked around with that charming smile and asked, "Arthur, can I help you?"

I almost went through the floor. Everything fell. I forgot all about what was on my mind.

A few days later, the fellows asked if I asked her. I said, "If you want somebody to ask her, why don't you ask her!"

The brother, William Riggs, had moved to Trinidad, seven boys and five girls. The boys teamed up together, and we became a force to deal with. We had a baseball team, and nobody could beat us. Sometimes at home, we would play with one another. Sometimes we would run short of a player, so Dina Riggs would fill in. She would play on the other side against me. Most of the time, I would be the pitcher. Here came Dina, hair standing straight up on her head, dress touching nowhere but on her two shoulders. Tall, skinny, and ugly Dina would say, "Throw it, you little red bastard, I'm going to hit it." I wound up and threw one at her. The very next ball I threw, she hit. The boys miss it on purpose. Dina slid into second base. "You little red bastard," she said, "I told you I was going to hit it." I was getting a little fed up with all this name-calling, everybody laughing was at me. Here she came again. She had the bat drawn back you would think she was batting the other way. Dina said, "Throw it, you little bastard." I got the old rag ball and squeezed the ball so that it would sail. I threw it right at her head, and she ducked out of the way. Dina said, "Why, you little SOB, you trying to hit me." She dropped the bat. She was coming at me and said, "This is all I wanted so I can whip your ugly ass." I'll be damned if I didn't fight her dirty; she would have whipped my hind parts. The boys broke it up. She went to the house crying because I hit her in the stomach. Now I felt like an ass. I had gone against all my mother's teaching. Mother said, "Son, you don't fight and beat women." A few days later, I begged her pardon, and we made up.

One day, I rode down by the ditch bank where there were a lot of juicy plums on the ground. I was on my knees eating plums and filling my hat when soon I heard a familiar voice. "Hey there, old damn nigger." It was Dina Riggs. She had a nasty mouth. "Bring me some of those plums."

"Me?" I said. "If you want some, you damn sure better come and get them."

"You know I'm afraid of snakes."

"Thank God, you're afraid of something."

"Come on, old boy, bring me some of those plums."

I said, "I'll make you a deal. I'll bring you a hatful of plums, but you have to get out of those drawers."

Dina said, "What the hell you think? I'm going to pull my drawers off for a hatful of plums."

"Well, that's the only way you're going to get any."

Soon she gave in, but I was going to give her some anyway. I came out with a hatful, and she ate those plums like she was hungry. She ate all the plums and then she jumped up. "Why, you little red bastard, if you think you're man enough, come and get it."

We rolled in the grass, both of us laughing for about ten minutes. Dina said, "All right you win." After a few rounds, Dina didn't look so ugly. When everything was over, she looked at me and laughed. "You don't fuck any better than you pitch." I put her on my horse and carried her home. Every time I went to the plum orchard, soon Dina would show up. We ate a lot of plums that fall.

Every once in a while, we had to take someone down. We'd whip his hind part and then rub our pricks over his nose. I had my share. This time it was Blue, his brother Jack, my brother, and me. We held Blue down, whipped his tail, and then rubbed our pricks over his nose. Then we ran to the house. Pete was sitting there by the fire. We went in just like nothing happened. Two minutes later, Blue walked in. He wasn't the type to cry out. He would just swell up and sniff. Pete said, "Boy, what's wrong?" Blue said, "Old Pudding and them held me down and rubbed their pricks over my nose." Pete said, "What?" He grabbed a big board, and I knew that that meant a tail whipping. I beat Pete to the door. Pete hit at me and missed. I jumped from the door, over the porch on the ground, and down that dusty road to safety. Ollie didn't allow nobody to hit me, but Pete could get away with it a little because she believed in Pete and thought he was fair.

Blue and I went five miles down to another plantation to swim with another large family. After swimming, we thought we would check out the young ladies. The Minor family had a house full of beautiful young ladies, and I had my eye on one called Clarise Minor. Those older brothers made those young brothers run after us like we were something good to eat. We finally got away. We went back home and told what they did to us. All that week, we planned our strategy how we were going to get even. Early Saturday, Jack, Pap, my brother, and all seven of the Riggs boys, we had our army ready for battle. First, we engaged them in a ball game. Next, we would get even. So we crap up three, winner takes all. We shut them out. Oh, by the way, we carried Little Peter Riggs—he was older—to keep the old honest.

Soon the fight started. We took them by age; everybody took a man. My brother Pap they always said he was a dirty fighter, the boy didn't get a lick of Pap. Struck the first deadly blow to Bill Minor. Pap hit him in the nose. The boy fell up in the fence, and blood flew everywhere. I felt sorry for Bill. We didn't hate those boys. We had known them all our lives. So they put cold water on him to stop the bleeding. The fight resumed, and this time, it was my turn to take his younger brother, Paul Minor. If I didn't know Paul, I would have sworn that they switched a gorilla on me. Paul was about as tough as they came. Soon they broke us up, and boy was I glad. We collected our little door. It was getting late, and we had five miles to walk. We crossed over Old Mississippi River to a farmhouse. He sold us a half gallon of corn liquor for fifty cents. On our way, we stopped down the road and decided to take a little drink. They passed it around, and when they got to me, I said no. The boys said, "Come on, man, take a little. You came all the way down here to get even, you whipped that old damn nigger, now find time to celebrate."

"OK, OK." I took a little swallow. I didn't want any more. We started on our way.

About a hundred yards up the road, we came to a huge tree that had blown down across the stream. We decided to cross back over to save time. Everybody crossed over but me. Just that quick, that stuff had gone to my head. I stood there looking at that log and all that water running under that log. The fellows were saying, "Come on, man, it's getting late, and we have a long ways to go yet." I started across, got in the middle, missed that log, and went down in that cold water. When I came up, I had promised God and everybody concerned that I will never take another drink of nothing. I was a good swimmer, but the boys had to jump in to get me. That water was carrying me away. We still had three more miles to walk. I stopped by the Minors' home. They lived near us. She was a single mom who had a very attractive young lady and son about my age. She made me pull off my pants, and she gave me a pair of her son's clothes. I went home and didn't tell my mother why I fell in the water, and when we met at church, I gave her clothes back. I was working in the field when I saw Mother coming. She held up her hand for me to stop. I stopped, and I could see she was a little troubled. She said, "Son, they have caught your uncle, and he was arrested in Vicksburg."

Tension was back at the church. The Joneses were sitting on one side, laughing. "We're going to hang him." Mother was praying to God to save him.

Now, Boss Man was dead, but his youngest son just finished law school. He came to mother and told her not to worry: they aren't going to hang him. She told the rest of the family what he said so they could smile back at the Joneses, The Joneses didn't know what was going on. Cliff Adams was the young lawyer, and the judge was his godfather.

The courthouse was full, waiting to hear the judge sentence Bus to be hung. They were ready to testify, but the judge didn't let anyone take the stand. The judge asked Riggs, "Are you guilty?" Bus said, "Yassir!" The judge said, "Fourteen years if you give trouble, seven on good behavior." The Joneses said justice was not served.

Soon Pete sent for his brother Jim Stewart out of someplace close to Gulf Port, Mississippi. Jim moved to Saunders's plantation, right on the line dividing the two plantations across the Old Mississippi River, in the exact place where the white and black kids did their fighting, Jim Stewart's family consisted of five daughters and one son. I believe I'm right when I say Shimmie was the oldest. I'm calling them by the names I knew; their real names, if I knew them, I have forgotten. Next were called Nigg, Thelma, Little Buddie, Baby Sis, and Little Sister. I hope I am right about the order I have them in.

If I made a mistake, they knew the order and one jersey cow. His wife said, "I don't know who you love more, me or the cow." Jim said, "I love you both, you because you gave me the kids and the cow helps me feed them."

Shimmie married my schoolmate Saul McSimpson, one of the boys who used to help us fight. She moved to Trinidad in the same house Martha Riggs, her aunt, lived in. Shimmie and I grew pretty close, so close she used me to see another one of my schoolmates, P. C. Flowers. When she wanted me to do her dirty work, Shimmie would say "Come here, cuz!" with a big smile on her face. "I want you to tell fat boy I want to see him." She meant PC and I went. I was the go-between. I prayed, "God, forgive me for helping break up that man's marriage." I was closer to PC than I was to Saul. One day, Saul came home looking for dinner, and Shimmie and PC were gone. I never saw them again.

My buddy was looking Thelma over, and I was looking over Baby Sis. The house where they lived, the kitchen was a large room out back from the house. When we wanted to see them, we would ride by the house. That was the OK for them to take their bath. In the summertime, all the farmers sat on the front porch to tell their tales, so they would come out behind the kitchen.

We had a little problem. Baby Sis had a dog, and every time we rode by the house, that old dog would run out after us. I told my partner that sooner or later that dog was going to betray us. So we set up a plan to get rid of the dog. My partner rode by first, and I waited till the dog got out good, running behind my friend. I came out along riding that red stallion that was as mean as a junkyard dog. Soon I heard that dog holler out. That was the end of Baby Sis's dog. Jim Stewart sent me a word that he was going to shoot me if I came riding by there again. Ollie sent him words, "If you hurt my son, I will have Cliff to lock your ass up and throw away the key." Mother told me, "Son, don't ride on that side anymore. If you have any cotton to be picked, you call Jim Stewart's family. He would pick you a bale in half a day, one bale of Big Bowl Rucker in August, when the son have those buds big and fluffy. Thirteen hundred pounds of seed cotton gave you a five-hundred-pound bale of cotton. If you were picking DPL, you would have to pick fifteen hundred pounds. Now let me explain a little more clearly to you. A Big Bow Rucker had more lint cotton. Less seeds. DPL had more seeds, less lint. So a wise farmer would plant both; if seeds were high that year, you made more, and if lint was high, you would make more money.

Adams would hire people to come pick his cotton. You go to town and get a truckload of people. Before you pull off, someone would drive up beside you and say, "One dollar a hundred and ice water" on every end. A few seconds later, your truck would be empty. You're paying the same price, but the ice water made the difference. I'm telling this so the young black men and women can understand the hardships their parents came through. Just ice water was a luxury. We would take a fifty-gallon barrel, fill it with water, and drop fifty pounds of ice in it for the people to drink. I couldn't pick much cotton. Sometimes, if a farmer had his crop under control, he would pick cotton for the white farmer to make him a few dollars on Friday and half of Saturday.

So fellows with a big family could make eighteen or twenty dollars on Friday and half of Saturday. Twenty dollars then was equal to a hundred dollars today.

Sometimes when mother would go out, she could pick close to four hundred pounds herself. My Uncle Steve said, "Boy, you can't pick much cotton. I want you to be the weight boy, to weigh the cotton." My responsibility was when that cotton was sent to the gin, I would have a five-hundred-pound bale of cotton. Adams would pay off by my figures. Sometimes I would have fifteen or twenty people picking cotton. I would help my mother until someone called out "weigh man," then I would put my little bit in her sack, so she would be ready to weigh up.

Sometimes these families would have three or four young ladies to rest up, and they would send them up to the cotton house for ice water. "OK, Bro Fox sitting in his cotton house going over his figures." I need two hundred pounds of cotton for myself, one hundred for my mother, one hundred for me. One day, this family had a young lady about fourteen. I was fifteen and a half. She came for a bucket of ice water. Bro Fox looked her over. So I popped the question to the young lady. Her answer was no before I asked. She went to walk away, and something came to Bro Fox. I offered her one hundred pounds of cotton. She turned around. "You're going to give me one hundred pounds of cotton? You're sure?" I said, "As sure as I stand here." "OK," she said. In the cotton house old Bro Fox went, and had him a beauty rolling eye red. After the picking was over, she went on to take the ice water to her parents. That evening, it was pay time and Adams paid off by my figures. The young lady drew more money than her mother. Right in front of the white man, her mother said, "Young man, you have something mixed up. You know my daughter didn't pick more cotton than me. Dad looked at her and said, "I say shut up." Boy, was I glad. Her mouth shut up like a clam's.

I knew all the good cotton pickers. Stewart and I took twenty from the white man. My Uncle Steve told me, "Boy, I know what you doing, that white man's going to catch you, but so far you've been hitting the mark." Then every time the mother of the young lady saw me, she would shake her fist at me.

One day I met this long-legged beauty, Joe Phillip's youngest daughter. She stole Old Pudding's heart. I had to pump my brood with car pump—that's some of the words the boys used in those days. I played the brother game. She had a brother my age, but soon her old man peeped my hole card. I had to ask to come to see her or I wouldn't get to see her, and I wasn't about to let that happen. I stayed away for two weeks. I was afraid to face that big man. He was a deacon in my church. His wife was one of the mothers of the church. They knew me from the time I was about four years old. I knew they liked me, but when you're going to ask one of those farmers to come and see his daughter, there had to be a lot of liking.

Mother gave me a good lift. She said, "You are going to have to face him sooner or later. He's not going to turn you down because you are my son. Who else could he let come see her if he turns you down? You are one of the finest and most handsome young man around here, well disciplined too."

The young lady sent me word through her sister Maude Riggs, Little Peter Riggs's wife, that everything was OK. Boy, you talking about a load being lifted off a young man's heart, it was mine. So I went up there; they were very nice to me and laid down all the rules. I didn't break one. The last thing he told me was, "If any thing happen to her, don't tell me it ain't you 'cause ain't nobody else coming here. If you take her away, you bring her back the same way." Wouldn't that be a good thing today? I thought so.

In those days, Wednesday day or night you could come see her, but at nine o'clock you better be ready to go. I had it a little better than the rest of the boys. I could stay till ten o'clock. The boys asked me, "What you use on that old man?" I just said good home training.

Soon they left the country and moved uptown. Saturday and Sunday you had to put on your best clothes and tie, go get her, bring her to the movies, and be back home by eleven o'clock. If you did those things, you were a fine young fellow. We fellows would meet going to the movies, take her home by eleven o'clock and kiss her good night, then pull your hat off and run like hell to the nightclub where the Duval girls were, ringing and twisting till the sun came up the next morning.

Ran down to Will Adam's house, got me a ride out in the country, fed my mule, lay down to go to sleep till ten o'clock, and I was ready. Right up till Saturday sundown, sometimes I would sleep behind the plow. One day, Mother said, "Son, if you don't stop going to sleep behind the plow, we won't have any cotton because you're plowing it up."

"Wow, I'm sleepy, I'm sure going to bed early tonight."

Around four o'clock, I had gained a new life. Here came Colombia Riggs say, "Man, there's a party going on tonight, want to go?"

I'd say sure. The next day I was telling myself the same lie: I'm going to bed tonight.

One night, Colombia Riggs and I were at a party. The fellows got a little jealous because the girls were paying a little more attention to us. We dusted them right fast. We looked around, and here came four more. Colombia said, "What do you think?" I said, "I think we need to get the hell out of here." Colombia said, "I'm thinking the same thing."

I don't know if any of you ever been in the country—no moon shining, clouds covering the stars, you can't see your hand before your face. You're walking along, you knew where you were going, but all at once you walk out of the cool normal air into warm air. Your hair stands straight up on your head, tickling down your back. You want to run, but you don't see anything. About twenty-five yards later, you walk back into a normal temperature. Some nights

I had to run back in the door, looking like something was going to grab me before I could get in the house. The old people used to say that there were evil spirits walking up on earth.

I believe there was something one night. I was riding along, talking with Colombia. All at once, when we entered into those hot airs, my horse started acting funny. His ears straight ahead soon we came back into the normal air. By this time, I was in church, a junior deacon was on the usher board. One Sunday, they decided to have a church anniversary. The ushers at Mount Pilgrim Baptist Church had a program. Street Phillips was mistress of ceremony, Viola Johnson did the welcome, and I was to follow with a response. After the prayer meeting, the spirit was high, you could hear those sisters' shoe heels on the hardwood floor. It sounded like a trap drum—*tap tap tap tap*—not an offbeat. The church was crowded, standing room only. A very little of that the windows were up, people standing on whatever they could find so they could look in. The door stood open on the porch, and all the churchgoers from near around were there, and the pulpit were full of preachers. Sequna Reed prayed the opening prayer, and the mistress of ceremony introduced Volia Johnson, Jack and Blue's sister. She stood before all these people and spoke like she was sitting at her dinner table. The crowd went wild and gave her a standing ovation. Soon the crowd fell silent you could have heard a rat piss on cotton. Soon she said, "Next response will be Master Arthur Barnett."

I walked down two steps into the deacon's pen. My heart was beating at a rapid pace. Pete Riggs was the first one to shake my hand. "All right, boy," he said. My sweetheart's dad was next to shake my hand. When I finally stood to face the crowd, I cast my eyes to the right at my mother. She smiled and bowed her head. I knew what that meant. My great aunt hollered out, "All right, boy, this is your great aunt!" I cast my eyes to my left, and my sweetheart was seating in the second seat from the front, looking at me dead in the eyes. I said to myself, *I've got to come through, her mother and two sisters are on the program.* I finally spoke and the crowd roared. They stood up and clapped.

We had some good speakers to come behind us. Viola's brother Blue spoke on the duty of a deacon. Approximately eight people were on the program, and everyone was just as good. Anthony Reed put the program together. The spirit was high. We had a lot more programs, but this one couldn't be duplicated. I have a desire to write down what I said.

> Mistress of ceremony, honorable pastor, honorable visitors, Christian friends, and to whom it took to make up this great congregation, welcome. *Welcome* is the greatest word in the English language or the greatest word to extend your light of hospitality. When the first cable was laid across the Atlantic Ocean, the first message rescue was

"welcome." When Benjamin Franklin caught lighting and tamed it as a horse in harness and a team of oxen made it work for the American people, it was "welcome." So you see, "welcome" is either at the beginning of a job or the ending of one.

I was supposed to turn to her, grab her hand, and look straight at her. She stood and looked at me in the eyes with a smile that would tame a gorilla. She was a beautiful girl, my cousin. I said, "Sister Johnson, you have my prayers for your faithfulness, and continue with our Lord and Savior Jesus Christ. I also pray that you grow strong spiritually as well as physically. If you continue until the end, you shall wear a victorious crown. For these remarks, I thank you."

Soon my pastor stood up. Jim Henderson said his remarks after the program was over. Don't forget there were some heavy speakers to come after us. My preacher said, "Little Nootsy and Pudding laid the foundation for this program. This program can't be shackled." The church said a loud amen.

To hear those words coming from him really meant a lot. I will tell you a few things about him. That fall was Revival, and they had been singing and praying the whole week, and nobody had come to sit on the "moaners' bench." For this generation, I will explain the moaners' bench. They would sit a bench out in front of the church for the sinners to come and sit on so the church could pray for them to be saved.

This night Jim Henderson stood up and told the deacons to open the door to the church. There must be somebody out there. So he started walking to the door. The people came with him singing "Come to Jesus." Out in the country, most farmers would walk his wife to church. He would then stand outdoors and look through the window. When Jim Henderson came to the door, all the fellows ran but one, and his name was J. B. Collins. The preacher asked him his name, and he said J. B. Collins. The preacher then asked, "Are you J. B. Collins, son?" And he said, "Yes, sir." The preacher said, "Why don't you come in and let us pray for you?"

The church was still singing "Come to Jesus." Collins turned around to walk away. He reached in his pocket, got a cigarette, and put it in his mouth. When he struck a match to light it, the match blew up in his face, and he almost ran over the preacher. They baptized him that fall. Jim Henderson was a powerful black preacher.

After running a farm for years, I thought it was time to kiss the old mule good-bye. Bus was due home soon, so I got an older fellow to stay till Bus came. I told my mother that I would still look after her, so I went uptown and got a job at the hotel as head busboy. Green as the grass was I when I left. On the farm, I was making $7 a week. The fellow gave me the job that was gone to Monroe. After two weeks, he returned, and soon we had a little chat. He asked me was I making any money, and I said $7 a week. He said, "Boy, you better wake up."

He went to the other bellboy and asked for the list and brought it to me. This is where you make your money. The names on that list made my heart jump. It included phone numbers and hair color. Some of the wives of the richest men in town were call girls. I said, "You don't expect me to call these women?" He said, "If you want to make some money." I said, "What good is the money when they hang me?" He said, "You'll be OK."

So one Saturday night, two young salesmen came. "Hey, bellboy, do you have any women?" At first, I said, "No, I'm new here." They said, "Bellboy, you better wake up, every good bellboy has some women and liquor handy."

I said, "Wait a minute." I went in the next room and got my nerve up. I came back and said, "I think I may be able to help you."

"Good," they said, "one brunette and one blonde."

"Give me about fifteen minutes."

"OK."

I asked if they still wanted some liquor, and they said, "Yeah!"

The brunette was right downstairs. I thought every time I came in the cafeteria she would look straight at me. So this night I nodded my head and held up five fingers for the room number. She nodded back. I called this oilman's wife. It seemed like she was waiting for the call. I told her the room number. The next morning, in my stash was $7 apiece. When the salesmen checked out, they shook my hand and slipped another $8. This was more money in one night than I made legal in a month. I had my locker filled with liquor. If someone wanted a little snout, I had it for him. All at once, I was no longer the little green country boy. Now I was a city slicker with a pocket full of money, a locker full of liquor, and five rich white gals to call. All this for a lad who, two weeks ago, was trying to get his cotton in before the winter. At school, I had two popular young ladies as my contacts. Doris Turner and Wilma Huff were my two buddies. I was so popular at the school that the teachers came to the door when I was passing by. One said, "You must be that Pudding, interrupting my class with young ladies hanging out the window waving at me."

God saw which way this young man was headed, so he decided to put an end to it. One third Sunday, I asked to be off till twelve o'clock because I wanted to go to church. Foster was the owner. He said, "OK, you have someone to work in your place?" I said, "Yassir." And he said, "OK, pray for me." All the war was going on. I went to church and was back by eleven thirty. I was dressed well as usual. I had on a blue pin-striped suit with a chesterfield overcoat, a patch imitation belt in the back, a blue real brim hat, and a white shirt with a maroon tie. I came back to the hotel to relieve the other bellboy. I was standing by the fire when Foster walked in. He looked me over, walked all around me. Foster said, "Goddamn! I haven't seen a nigga dress like this in my life. You got to leave here."

I said, "Watch your mouth on that nigga stuff."

"We will rap as you're going to get the hell out of here."

"Give me my money!"

He said, "Come back tomorrow and get it."

The next morning at nine thirty, I showed up with a brown double-breasted suit with the hat to match. He wouldn't let me in to get my money. He sent it to the door. A week later, I had a real job, forty hours a week.

Now let's get back to Davis Ben. The Ransomes made up a large part of our family. My brothers, two of them, married two of the Ransome daughters. One of the Ransome sons married one of my sisters. If I had lived on the island, I probably would have gotten the youngest one named Mildred. Now back to my older brother, we called him Son Barnett and his beautiful wife Nig. If you went to Louisiana and didn't go by to see them, you missed a treat. She could tell you enough about their marriage that would have you laughing for a week. I'll give you one example. They were in Vicksburg, Mississippi, and went to the valley dry goods store. It was a very high-class store. They dealt straight out to New York for their goods. Only a very few people could afford to go there. He brought her a mink coat and a suit for himself. On their way down Washington Street, a white fellow pushed her off the street. My brother said, "Hey, peckerwood! I didn't push your wife." The white fellow said, "I didn't push her, but I'll whip the hell out of you." My brother told his wife, "Hold my coat until I put this SOB to sleep." The fight started, and the peckerwood was hitting him everywhere but under his foot. His wife said to him, "You said you were going to put the peckerwood to sleep, look's like he's going to put you to sleep!" Again my brother said, "Damn peckerwood won't be still." She said, "What the hell do you think you're fighting a telegram pole?" A few seconds later, the peckerwood made a mistake and let my brother catch hold of him. She said she knew the fight was over. My brother hit him, and he fell like a dead man.

While they were fighting, the white people gathered around, some cheering for the white fellow and some cheering for Son. After the fight was over, he stood there and said, "Damn SOBs, since I'm passing out ass whipping, are there any more that want to join in?" She said, "Put your coat on, you damn fool, before they kill both of us!"

Now that I'm fired from the hotel, I'm working at the sawmill at $18.75 every Saturday. I would give my mother $10. I didn't have any rent, no food to buy. I was living with my godmother. I came there after my sister moved to Los Angeles. In the middle of 1942, maybe in August, every Monday morning, you could see someone come to work waving his ticket on his way to LA. First, their brothers went to LA, then they sent back for their family. Every night at ten o'clock, the train station would be full. You'd see who was leaving, who was coming in. People from everywhere were coming to the little town, looking for work. If you wanted to work, you could find a job, but those who lived here were looking for something better. The white farmers said, "With all the niggers leaving, who gonna work the farms?" So they stopped selling tickets to LA. You had to get one to Monroe, then change to LA.

I was coasting along, didn't want to leave too early. I wanted to be sure the boss was coming soon. Sometimes when the work would run a little slow, the supervisor would come around and ask who wanted to go home. Especially on Monday morning, I would raise my hand. Bill Ross would say, "OK, Arthur, see you Wednesday." To hours, I could easily make my forty hours. I would catch a ride out in the country to help my mother and the old-timer I left her with. I gave her $10 a week, so if she needed help, she could hire some help. I had my little game going. I was doing a little shacking. The young lady did something that made me back away a little, not all the way. I was guilty of the same thing, but I didn't get caught.

All my friends were leaving, so I thought I would follow them. My mother and godmother got to me. My mother said, "Son, you are grown now, I can't tell you what to do or not to do, but I'm still you're mother. When you see a group running one way, you go back the other way because it might be trouble." My godmother said, "Amen. Why don't you go to Norfolk, where my husband's working at the Naval Base? He said they are really hiring people."

I guess because my mother gave me a lot of good advice, I took some and some I didn't. I took the most of them, but some I regret I didn't listen too. You can't beat a God-fearing woman, who always keeps her son's name up before God. I used to hear her talking late at night. I asked her one day, "Who were you talking to so late last night?"

She said, "Son, I was talking to the master on your behalf."

"If you don't let him sleep, why don't you let me sleep?" I asked.

She smiled and said, "Someday you will understand."

So I packed my little stuff in October, one Tuesday night. When the nine nineteen train came through, I boarded it. I left someone standing at the station whom I loved dearly—my childhood sweetheart. I didn't know what was ahead of me. My mother always told me, "Son, don't ever carry a man's daughter somewhere unless you have a place for her to lay her head." I didn't know where I was going to lay mine. I always say that was one mistake. When I got on the train, there were two more couples that I knew—Eleanor Hayes and Loleta Skinner and Horace and Hazel. They tried to get me to go to DC with them. That was two thirty Thursday, October 27, 1942, and I haven't heard from or seen them since. I have inquired about their whereabouts to no avail. I stood at the door, they went out, and we waved good-bye to each other. I turned around; the train was crowded with people, but they were all strangers to me. All at once, fear came over me. For some reason I felt all alone.

I mentioned this to another fellow some years ago. He said, "That was your last connection to home." I guess he was right. I sat down and I said, "Pudding, you have until seven thirty to grow up to be a real man because every decision you make will determine your future, whether it be good or bad." At seven thirty, I arrived in Norfolk. I caught a taxi to C Avenue. I don't remember the number now. The house has been torn down. Remember some pages back, I told about our church anniversary and the lady that prayed the open prayer. She was the first face I met. I stayed there until Anthony came. Her husband was the same fellow that put the program together, and he and I went to see if I could find myself a place to stay. Thanks to the Almighty, I found a home right across the street from them. Mrs. Mackie's was $6.50 a week, room and board. The next morning at five thirty, I rose Luke Williams, my godmother's husband, and we caught the trolley car to the naval base. I stood at the gate, and Roy Hughs came out to hire. He said, "Good morning, men. I will ask you do you want to work, if so stand over there." He called four fellows and asked them where they lived. Two were from North Carolina, Roger and Ton Vinson. The next was from the Eastern Shore. The fourth man he turned down was from Norfolk. I found out later why he was turned down. If you were from Norfolk, you wouldn't work. I found out later they were right. He turned to me. "How about you, young man?" With energy I said, "Yassir." Hughs asked, "Where are you from?" I said, "Louisiana." "OK," Hughs said, "that's all for today, fellows, come back tomorrow." I arrived Thursday morning at seven thirty, and by eight thirty Friday morning, I had a job. Ollie Riggs's prayers had reached here long before I arrived.

I joined a gang and went out to work. The man in charge noticed me working and came over to me. "Hey, young fellow, where you from?" I said, "Louisiana." He said, "I thought there was something different about you, you don't mind working." I said, "I've been working all my life on a farm." He said, "That speaks for itself." He asked, "Do you mind if I call you 'Louisiana'?" I said I didn't. That evening, when we went in, the supervisor asked him, "How about the new man?" Hawkins said, "Louisiana does more than three of those fellows."

I was trying to become established as a good worker with good attendance. Soon I was transferred to another gang, a group of mixed ages, younger and older. The supervisor was Brown, a big, heavy white fellow. I thought he was a kind fellow, and he seemed to take a liking to me. I learned he liked funny jokes, so I kept him laughing. He also called me Louisiana, and I worked ten hours a day, six days a week, and eight hours on Sunday.

I was trying to build my annual and sick leave up. I was a long way from home by myself. The families from my home left and went to Detroit. They wanted me to go with them, but I stayed where I was. If I was late for my job, my supervisor would hit my clock for me and stay and wait for me. Sometimes

I would almost be out of breath. Sometimes the streetcar would break down and stop the whole line. Sometimes I would walk a mile, and he would wait at the clock for me. Sometimes I would be running, and Brown would say, "Slow down, I've already hit the clock for you. I knew you were coming. You're not like the other fellows, work two days a week."

Now I have established myself as a good employee, six months without a day off. I really enjoyed going to work. If I got there early, I could go to the cafeteria, where a lot of young ladies were. These older fellows had plenty of money, cars—a little guy didn't have a chance. Going to work in the dark and coming home in the dark, I didn't know any young ladies. About five or six months trouble in the flesh. One night I couldn't sleep. I got up the next morning and went to the job. I mentioned it to the fellows on the job. "Why did I do that!" They laughed all day long; they told the supervisor, and he even joked he was almost sixty and he was doing OK. "How old are you, Barnett?" he asked.

"Me," I said, "nineteen."

One of the young men, Mitchell, spoke up, "If you want to go with me tonight, I know where some ladies are!"

I said "OK."

Mitch said, "It's going to cost you $5."

I said OK. I said to one of the fellows, "Five dollars, all I'm used to paying for is a hatful of juicy plums or one hundred pounds of cotton."

One of the fellows said, "You're not in the cotton fields anymore, you're in the city."

That night, Mitch and I went to this house. I don't remember the number, but I sure do remember the street—Wood Street. Whores alley I found out later. There were two young ladies there sitting by the fire, and Mitch made his play right away. Fifteen minutes later, I'm still sitting there. Soon the young lady said to me, "Are you new to this?"

I said yes, and she caught me by the hand and led me in a dark room. She got out of her clothes. "Come on, honey," she said. I dropped my pants, ain't nothing standing up yet. She said, "Come on, honey." She grabbed hold of it. The more she pulled on it, the limper it got. After about five minutes, she asked me, "How old are you?" I said, "Nineteen." She said, "Ain't that a damn shame, young man dead already." I laughed and gave her the $5. She said, "Whenever you can get it up, you can come back, your $5 is still good."

Soon my buddy came out. Mitch asked, "Are you OK?" I said yes, and he said, "Let's go." On our way home, I told Mitch what happened, and he laughed at me all the way home. Mitch said, "You hadn't had any in six months, you come over here, paid your money, and didn't do nothing."

The next morning, I was a little late. When I arrived, everybody was laughing at me. The supervisor was joking. I had told a joke about Grandpa. I told them one day I had a young lady around the side of the house. She was getting ready to get out of her clothes. I looked around and there stood Grandpa. Grandpa said, "Say . . . say . . . say . . . Pudding, are you going to do something to that gal?" I said, "No, Grandpa." Grandpa said, "Hold my stick and let me." He was ninety. My supervisor hadn't forgotten that joke. He said, "Maybe Barnett should have had Grandpa." For one week, I was the laughing boy. The next Monday morning, Mitch said, "Barnett's thang had more sense than you, that girl is burnt up with the disease. The city picked her up, and they put her in the hospital." I said, "Thank the Lord, this is the end of this." Until this day, strange women haven't been my thing. I wanted to be around you, see how you conducted yourself. I liked to see you sometimes in public to see if you were a drunk. I didn't care how good you looked. If you were a drunk or a nasty talker, I didn't care for those types of ladies.

So I teamed up with two brothers, Roger and Tom. Roger was married, Tom wasn't. We would dress and walk down Church Street. Church Street was crowded with people from every walk of life. We would sometimes walk down Church Street. I was standing on the corner waiting for the light to change when Tom said, "Look, Barnett, at this pretty lady."

I looked around. It was a young lady who lived across from my sister when I was living with her. She was on the run from the law. Her husband beat her, and she liked to kill him with a switchblade. I know it has been over sixty-five years, but I won't give her name. So we moved on down the street to the metropolitan drugstore. They had a little place in the back where you could dance. That night, two young men from Suffolk, Virginia, were there. One had a very foxy lady. I tried to move in on him. I gave her the nod, and she responded. I walked down in front of the store. Soon she came, and we had a few words. The young man soon broke it up. He took her to the back where they were dancing. As soon as she got back there, the music was playing. One of those fellows with the long frock and the big wide hat grabbed her, and they started dancing. It was one of those mad pieces. They were so close they looked like they were glued together. This young man couldn't stand it any longer. They started a little scuffle, but his friend jumped in between them. The friend said, "Man, we came up here to have some fun, not to go to jail." Someone said, "Police!" and his friend pushed him out the side door. Here came this black cop. He walked up, grabbed the young man, and hit him so hard with that stick he broke it in two. He took the other part and just pushed it in his side. The young man was crying, "Mister, please don't kill me." Blood was all over him. The young lady said, "Mister, please don't kill him." He dragged him right by me. Everybody was getting out of the way but me. He almost stepped on my foot.

I was so angry with that black officer I said, "If that SOB ever cross me, I will kill him."

You better be careful what you say out of your mouth because the devil is listening. Less than one month later, this man and I also came face-to-face and only God knew the outcome. I had now moved to Hunter Street. I had someone kiss on me every evening when I came home. I knew the young man wasn't all there, so I figured a way to stop the kissing. I gave him a pint of ice cream every evening. When he would start to me, I would hand him the ice cream. He would thank me and pat me on the back. His mother thought that I didn't like her son. I had nothing against the young man. I just didn't want him kissing me.

I moved to 757 C Avenue, and the homeowner was W. C. White. I came home, and after washing up, I sat on the front porch for a few minutes. A young lady came by. Her name was Helen Kennedy. She spoke and I spoke back. She walked by me and looked back. I said, "Hey, come here." She turned around and we talked. She said, "I'm on my way to the store for my mother, I'll be back." And she did. A few minutes later, I slipped her up to my room to talk a little more. I didn't know my landlord was looking at me.

The next day, when I came in, Mr. White said, "Arthur, you didn't think I saw you last night." I went to say something, but he said, "Everything's OK, you kept it quiet. I want to warn you about her father. He's an old dirty man. Nobody in the neighborhood likes him. She is a fine you lady, so is her mother, but nobody cares for that dirty rascal." I had no idea that this was the man I spoke to a month ago and said, "If he ever cross me, I would kill him." Remember, I told you that Bus told Addlee, "If you ever cross me again, I will kill you"? Now his nephew had said the same words thirty years later. Satan was still at work. One week later, he came to the house looking for me. I was at work. When I came in, Mr. White said, "Good evening, Arthur!" He then asked me if I was in any type of trouble. I said, "No, sir. Why, Mr. White?" Mr. White asked, "Are you sure? I work downtown where all the lawyers are, if you need one, I will get you one. The reason I asked you is because that dirty man I told you about has been here looking for you."

I said, "Thank you, sir!" I went upstairs saying to myself, *What the hell he want with me?* Somebody must have told him his daughter was coming around here to see me. I washed up, dressed, and said to myself, *I was going to see what the hell he wanted with me.* I had never been to the house. On my way out the door, I turned around and put my .25 automatic pistol in my pocket. I went around to the house and knocked on the door. He was sitting at the dinner table. According to his daughter, I knocked on the door and he started to get up. She said I fell on her mind, and something told her to get up quickly and go to the door. Her father started to the door. She said, "It's OK, I will open it." She came to the door and opened it. I saw she was afraid. She slammed the door behind her and rushed to me to put her hand over my mouth. Please don't say a word, let me and Mother handle this. I went back downstairs. She went with me. "Mother and I will take care of him," she said. "You stay out of it."

As I got older, I looked back over my life, and I think I would be justified calling myself a young fool. Let's say he came to the door to see me. I see him. I'm not going to let him do me like he did that young man. Suppose I had hurt him, the law would say that you went there to harm him, on purpose. Why did you have that gun in your pocket? The devil sent me there, but God was there ahead. That's the only way I could see it.

This is why I hate to see a young man with a gun. It'll make him think he's bigger than he is. On the job, I was learning how to shoot crap. I had never had a pair of dice in my hand. I had the dice. I was shooting. Everybody was picking up but me. Soon James Grady spoke up. James said, "I'm getting damn tired of you fellows taking this man's money." He said, "Shoot, I'll tell you when to pick up. I broke those guys, and they got mad at James." The guys said, "You're telling this damn nigger from Louisiana how to beat us." They got hot, but they knew better than to grab James. One fellow from New York jumped at James. James threw him so hard he threw his shoes off his feet. I said to myself, *Damn, I'm sure glad he's on my side.* One day, he asked me, "Do you have a special girl to take out Saturday and Sunday to the movies?" I said, "No, I'm playing catch them if you can. If I catch one, OK. If not, it's OK too!" James said every man ought to have a special girl to call on Sundays. I agreed. When I was home, I had one. James said, "This weekend I'm giving a party over to my girl's house, come on over. There's a young lady from my home I grew up with. She's here from Little Washington, North Carolina. You better catch her before she gets city slick."

My two buddies and I went to the party, and sure enough, there sat a cute little young lady. He introduced us. They all started dancing. Some of them drank beer; I noticed she didn't, but she loved to dance. I couldn't dance, only the slow pieces. I sat over in the corner like old Bro Fox checking the farmer's henhouse out. I said, "You guys can dance with her all you want, but when she goes home, I'll be the one to take her." It wasn't far, just right across the street. When the party was over, she came and sat beside me. I brought her home, and sixty-one years later, I'm still bringing her home. That's my wife, Lillie Virginia Barnett. She was going to Elizabeth City College. She only came home on the weekends, so I had a lot of time to play the field while she was in college. Exactly, one year from the date that I arrived in Norfolk, I was married to her. I wrote Mother and told her what happened. She said, "You marry that girl. You said she didn't have a mother or father, you have messed up that young lady's life. You marry her and bring her and my grandson so I can see her. God won't bless you if you do something crooked."

Two months later, Uncle Sam called me in the army. The actual duty date was December 7, 1943. I had ten days leave when I finished my basic training. I came to see her and didn't see her again until three years later.

I want to back up a little. Two weeks before I got married, I came home one day, and Mr. White was standing on the porch as usual, with a big smile on his face. Before I could speak, Mr. White said, "Arthur, a beautiful young lady has been here looking for you. She's about your complexion with a gold crown in front of her mouth. She said she was from your hometown. Do you know her?" I said, "Yes, I do!" I'm sure you heard me mention those women twisting at the nightclub, those devil daughters. Well, this was one. I don't care what she did. You give her five minutes with you, you would remember no more whatever she did. She was like a wasp in your pocket of your shirt. She would hug you, kiss you every second she was with you. Her name was Kizzie Perry, and if she had arrived here a month before, I promised my wife and family that I was going to marry her. I don't know what would have happened. I'm quite sure I would have taken the same path I took.

Now I was in the army. Three busloads left Norfolk. Camp Lee was our first stop. The barracks we moved into was on restriction, so we couldn't go to the cafeteria. The next morning, they gave us our uniforms. When I went through the line, the PFC said to me, "I have just the uniform for you." He wasn't lying; it was made to fit me. Hard finished goods, nobody had a uniform like it. Soon they called us out for shots, five shots at one time. Boy, my arm was sore. It started snowing a little. They called us out to police the area, but we didn't know what *police* meant—simply pick up the paper off the ground. It was cold. I found a warm place in the boiler room, so I sat there, cold arm hurting. Soon a PFC in charge came in and caught me. He gave me a shovel and a ton of coal to move. He said, "When you finish, you can go in." My buddies got buckets and helped me move the coal to the coal bin.

I found out right then that disobeying orders wasn't for me. The next morning, when they came for inspection, our barracks was spotless. The captain asked, "How long you fellows been here?" We answered, "Two days." And he said we had done a good job. We're off restriction, and over to the canteen we went, but those fellows that were stationed there had all the young ladies tied up. We said we were going to stick together. Boy, were we wrong. They picked one or two every day and sent them to a different part of the country. At the end of the week, they called me out, put me with 250 strangers, and shipped me to Indiantown Gap, Pennsylvania. It was up in the hills. Cold winds stayed at thirty-five miles per hour with snow.

I was in the first platoon. In every formation, I had to be the first man out. Standing at attention were more than 250 men to dress right dress, ready front, full dress. I soon could tell the southern country boys from the city boys. The city boys couldn't get out of bed at five thirty in the morning unless he was a paperboy or worked with a milk truck. I had been getting up at five thirty all my life. Out in the country, if the sun caught you in bed, you were considered a lazy man. After our basic training was up, we moved to a new camp in Staten Island, New York. The captain said, "I want you to look good. Your first impression determines who you are." Marching through the city, 1,200 strong, we were the leaders in front, and I was the pivot man. The streets were full of people. They were coming out, stars waving, mostly an Italian community. The sergeant said, "Sound out, cadence count, one-two-three-four, one-two-three-four, Sergeant. Sound of cadence, Ain't no use in calling home, Jodie got your wife and gone, one-two-three-four, one-two-three-four." Just think how that sounded with 1,200 men, all at once. Those people thought that was the funniest thing they had ever heard. A group of men, we were the first soldiers there.

Some 1,200 men were singing, coming under a new post commander. He and his assistant were standing there watching. He had never heard the new cadence count, and boy, did he love it. He asked the captain, "Where did they get that from?" And the captain said, "They made it up." I don't think he had ever seen that many black men together. We got in our new barracks, and a half hour later, they blew the whistle. We all came out getting ready to eat at the new mess hall. You will never guess what we saw coming: fifty black women that made us look like Boy Scouts. When they got up to us, they did a right-face salute. That meant they all turned their face to us and saluted us. We stood at attention and saluted them back. Some 1,200 men were smiling at fifty beautiful black women, all around nineteen to twenty years old. We joined in right behind them. Now listen to the new cadence. All at once, someone came up with this: "Ain't no use looking back, I'm going to get me one of these WACs, one-two-three-four, one-two-three-four, hup hup." Those girls laughed so much their formation broke up. The lieutenant was laughing.

You get a group of young men out there by themselves from all walks of life, from different parts of the country, and you'll be surprised at the things they can come up with. We had some wicked ones too! As far as I can give an account of, we had to save men in our company. They kept their Bibles with them.

We, the 624th port company boys, had a lot of fun in Staten Island. Our battalion was made up of 625th, 626th and 627th. Those were our assistant company. After approximately five months of training there, those young ladies fixed up our papers to go overseas. There were a lot of tears shed the day we moved out. I want to tell you who was shedding. We moved to Camp Killma, New Jersey. We didn't have any passes, no nothing. Our lieutenant went to the post commander and told him that his men needed to have passes. We were there a week. Our lieutenant said, "My men want to go AWOL, and the post commander said OK." Before we left that station, we had a captain we knew didn't like black people. So we signed a petition to get rid of him. When the first sergeant got the paper, the first lieutenant called a formation. He asked, "Do you fellows know what you have done? You don't sign a petition against an officer in the army. They will court-martial every one of you." About a hundred scratched their names off the list. The rest left their name there. My name was the fifth on the list, so they sent it to the post commander. He called a meeting, and we got rid of him. Captain Clark chose a new first lieutenant. Jannett was his name, and all the fellows liked him. But we still had one more—both of them were from Oklahoma. James from Mississippi caught him one day and started to whip the hell out of him. The post commander told us, "It's bad enough that you have to leave your families to go overseas to fight for your country, and the one who's leading you hates you. No, he will not go with you."

At Camp Killma, I got a pass to come back to Staten Island to see a young lady I met while I was there. I will say a few things about her. She was a well-developed young lady and beautiful. She fell in love with me. I thought a lot of her, but I couldn't cross that line. She was a virgin. I didn't want to mess up her life and mine too! I had to turn cold turkey. That's army talk, cold turkey. The last night I was there, I told her and her family that I wouldn't be back. They all broke down in tears. I really felt rotten inside. On our last night in America, we were restricted, no passes. We moved out six o'clock the next morning. My buddy, Charles Anderson, a tall handsome fellow, loved to go out with me because he drank and I didn't, and he knew I would keep him in line. He was a really good dancer, light on his feet. They had taken our summer uniforms. We had on winter uniforms in July, and we were really mad. They knew what they were doing, but we didn't.

That night, Charles and I crawled almost one hundred yards and got under the fence in the dark so the guards wouldn't see us. We went across the street to the USO, and as soon as we walked in the door, all the GIs and young ladies turned and looked at us. They knew what was going on. That was our last night in the States, and they treated us royal. As soon as the music started playing, my buddy had the floor. The young ladies were having themselves a ball with him. I had to catch all the slow ones because I danced like a fellow with two left feet. Soon the MPs walked in. They said, "Don't you know you aren't supposed to be out here?" I said, "Yes, but since it's our last night, I thought we would have a little fun." The MPs said, "I'm going to have to take you fellows in." The GIs got around those MPs and asked, "Why you want to make things miserable for these fellows?" I spoke up. "When they close up, why don't you come, give us a ride back to camp." They agreed. They closed at eleven o'clock. Every USO had a live band. Their closing song was "Good night, sweetheart, until we meet tomorrow." The GIs lined up one side, and the young ladies were down the other. We walked down between them, kissing and hugging the young ladies, shaking hands with the GIs. Some of the young ladies had tears in their eyes. Estella Ashby, who lived in East Orange, New Jersey, said to me, "If you spend the night, I will have you there at camp at five thirty." Those MPs said, "They're going back to camp." As good as she looked, if the MP hadn't showed up, I sure was going to spend the night.

I was still trying to hold the marriage banner up. Trouble in the flesh was mounting. It was hard. When so many beautiful young women were coming by, smiling at you, only God could save you. I wasn't calling Him to save me. I had only been to New York a few times, but I heard about many things happening to GIs. Meet a young lady, go home to spend the night, and wake up the next morning married to her. She had someone fix the papers with a fake signature. One GI went to bed with one and had to come back to camp in a dress. He met the MP and told them he was a GI. The MP wanted to know. "Where's your uniform?" Don't no GIs in our army wear a dress unless he is a WAC. Sergeant Harris of Alabama said he meet this pretty young lady at the bar. They had a few drinks, and soon they went upstairs. He was so anxious he couldn't get out of his pants quick enough. Soon this sissy got in bed. Sergeant jumped up and said, "What the hell is going on?" The sissy said, "What you see, that's what's going on." Sergeant said, "You've got the wrong man." The sissy jumped up and said, "You're going to do something before you leave here. I've been giving you my liquor, brought you to my pad, you're going to do something." Sergeant said, "I'm going to whip the hell out of you." He swung on the sissy and knocked her down. The sissy got up and whipped the hell out of him. The landlady had to pull the sissy off him. So as you can see, I didn't want anything like that happening to me.

On August 2 at six thirty, we left New Jersey and went to New York. The old British cattle ship was waiting for us. It looked like every young lady in New York was standing there waving good-bye. Moments like that, I don't care how long you live, you'll never forget. The very first name they called was Arthur Barnett. You show your dog tags, your ID, all the company leads. Approximately two hours later, we were on our way. One GI jumped overboard and tried to swim to shore. The wool suit got wet. He was about to drown when he yelled out, "Save me, somebody!" A British sailor jumped overboard and saved him. Some of the fellows said, "Damn fool ought to drown." I don't know, that fellow might have been me. That said that. I told my mother, "Don't worry, I would be back." It got pretty shaky a few days out. Remember when I told you how mad we were when we had to put on our winter uniforms in July? Well, four days out, we were pulling out overcoats, long drawers, and whatever else we could put on. When you'd go up on deck, the water was so cold it foamed like soapsuds. The water was jumping over the deck, and one fellow almost got washed overboard. We left with one ship, but the next morning on each side, we could see ships as far as we could look. We were in the middle.

I can't describe in pencil and paper the conditions we lived in, on that ship. For fourteen days, going across the Atlantic Ocean, we ate and slept in the same place—an open space with tables. Twelve men sat to one table, and two men with buckets would go up to the galley twice to get food. One day, they sent rotten boiled eggs, which we threw overboard. The meat tasted like they boiled it with no salt or pepper, real coarse meat. The sergeant said it looked like horse meat. We couldn't eat anything but bread and butter—four loaves of bread and a stick of butter for twelve hungry men. When night came, we tied our hammock over the table where we ate. I was the first man to go to the table. That put me upside the steel wall. That steel wall wore my hind parts out for fourteen days. On about the seventh day, they got a message that the Germans had a group of subs waiting for the convoy. We turned and headed to the North Atlantic. I thought going straight across water was rough enough. That North Atlantic, I didn't think some of those ships would make it, but they did.

One night, we were all sitting around talking about New York, some writing, some shooting dice, some playing cards, some swearing and cursing. But these two saved men, both named Brown, kept their Bibles, reading. All at once, we heard death charges going off all around the ship. The ship would shake at every charge. Lieutenant sent word downstairs to keep quiet, don't make any noise; the Germans were looking for the troop ship. For a few minutes, you could hear a rat piss on cotton. They wanted to sink the troop ship, where the men don't care how many or how much equipment you have. If you don't have anybody to use it, it's no good to you. All at once, Curtis Davis said, "No use calling on the Lord now, you didn't call on him in New York, when you were running those whores." Everybody turned to him and said, "Shut the hell up." I had made up my mind; if we got hit, I was going down with the ship. If you jumped overboard, you had three minutes before you froze to death. Your chances of being picked up were very slim. I saw something swimming alongside that ship. It looked like he wanted to eat up someone. It was half as long as the ship. The convoy wasn't going to stop and pick up anybody. Our mailman got so poor and weak when we got to England. They had to carry him off in a stretcher. I thought sure we would lose him. Steven Butler was his name.

These are just a few things that happened on that ship. After four days, we arrived in Liverpool, England. We arrived at about ten o'clock in the morning, and they kept us on the ship until dark. We were glad to see land. Some of the fellows kissed the ground. That night, we boarded a train. We traveled all that night, the next day, and until two thirty the next night. We arrived in South Hampton, England. Those loving cooks of ours made us hot cakes and spam at six thirty the next morning. You are talking about a hungry group of fellows.

When we were back home, we used to really talk about these cooks. Them damn fellows can't boil water. When we went through the line, they reminded us of our remarks. "No, cooks," we said, "you guys are the best cooks in the world, not only do you know how to boil water, you guys have learned how to make tea." A few days later, the Red Cross showed up with hot coffee and donuts, and you should have seen the beautiful black young lady who was driving it. She came right off the same street where I used to live. Her name was Mary Lamb. I didn't know her, and I never saw her again. The white soldiers were there before us and told the people we were like animals. "Don't trust your daughters with them. They have tails that don't come out until dark." They were right, only our tails came out in front, and those girls loved it. The 625th company wouldn't give their men a pass. The captain said there weren't any colored women over there.

Somebody wrote the post commander and told him what was going on. He called the whole regiment out, and from the way he talked to the captain, I felt sorry for him. He was from Georgia, but I won't trouble you with all the things he said to him. That evening everybody got a pass! Boy, everything went up. GI Joe, you know what I'm talking about. The Glenn Miller band was at the USO. You talk about dancing, those fellows really had a time. Those English girls were learning to jitterbug. Those black boys were teaching them. The white boys got mad, and they had a riot, if we didn't put a whipping on their hind part. The English soldiers joined us. The next couple of nights, no white boys showed up. A few days later, Eisenhower gave orders to ship us out. He said, "If they want to fight, send them where they can fight." We boarded a ship, and off to Normandy Beach we went. We got off the ship out in the channel, and a small craft took us ashore. We had twenty miles to walk inland. It was getting late, and they had a white line wide enough for men to walk. We had strict orders not to step outside that line. You might step on a mine, kill yourself, and someone else. We were walking at a rapid pace. We wanted to reach our destination before dark. That's when my second-in-command got tired. He was short—about five feet two—and with a ninety-pound pack on his back, a twenty-pound Springfield rifle, and a water bottle.

His name was Walter Bailey, and he was from Norfolk, just like I was. Bailey said, "Sarge, I don't think I can make it." I said, "You have to, don't step outside that line." I took his pack—ninety pounds—and put it on top of mine. Wesley Blakley from Florida took his rifle and carried it the rest of the ten miles. We arrived a little before sundown in a big field with an apple orchard. We dug in two feet in the ground and pitched a tent over it with two foxholes. We each had one can of hash, one pack of crackers, some instant coffee, and a helmet. We did everything with our helmet—wash up, heat our can of beans, and wore it on our head for protection. Soon we moved to a city called Roscoff in France. We found an old hotel right on the water, all bombed up and full of mines. One morning, we heard a loud boom. We thought the Germans had dropped a bomb. A mine that the Germans had left behind had gone off on our neighboring company and killed half of our friends. I had never seen so many dead people in all my life. We were assigned to Patton's Third Army.

In December 1944, the Germans had made a counterattack that almost destroyed the first army. They were headed to Le Havre, and we arrived there December 23. Before we left Roscoff, we were called to the Catholic Church. We thought we were going to service. After we came back to camp, the captain told us what the service meant—they were preaching our funeral. There is something I want to make very clear about the Red Ball Trucking Company. When they made a movie out of it, they had all white soldiers. Listen to me, I'm going to say this in plain words! There wasn't a white soldier in the Red Ball Trucking Company. They were all black. I met those fellows, loaded their trucks with ammo, and took food to the front lines. I rode in those trucks with those fellows. The Germans tried to stop them. They drove in a group of fourteen or fifteen at a time, for protection.

There's something else I haven't heard mentioned. A lot of women's sons, black soldiers, were hung in Europe. They sent messages to their parents, saying their son was missing in action. Now let me tell you why. The Germans were in France for four years before they were driven out. A lot of these women were in love with those Germans, and the Germans left them as spies. They found out that they could lie on a black GI and have him hung. Every weekend, some GI would have a pass to go to town. On Monday, a white MP with a woman would go to every black company. They would call you out to line up. She would pick you out, the MPs would arrest you, and Eisenhower would sing for you to be hung. I know this for a fact.

If you thought you shouldn't be afraid, you were greatly mistaken. You knew you didn't do it. You didn't have a pass that weekend. But you're still afraid. You knew there was something wrong, but there was nothing you could do to stop it. But God stopped it. She picked out the wrong man. He was on duty that night. His officer stood up for him. This man and I were on duty the same night, and then they started investigating the dirty system.

Now we are in Le Havre, moving through the city in a snowstorm, looking for a place to set up camp. Soon we saw a big building. Everybody was happy. When we arrived there was no top, but the captain said it was better than sleeping on the cold ground. So we pitched a tent inside. You'd be surprised what a group of men could do together with nothing. My buddy and I, the only place we could find was a large bathroom, but it had a top on it. A little water was inside. We dried it up and made us a heater. We got a pipe and broke out a windowpane so the smoke could go out. Soon it got warm. We had two blankets apiece. We put two on the floor and covered up with the other two. I had never slept so close to a man in my life. We wrapped up in those blankets so tight you would have thought there were two sissies. Later that night the wind changed and blew the smoke back in the room. The next morning when we awoke, we couldn't see each other, God was with us. The door had a two-inch gap at the bottom, so the fresh air kept the smoke above our noses. My buddy looked at me and said, "Boy, that was a close call." My mother and my church kept my name up before the Lord I knew that. The next day, we were busy trying to get things in order. A little bit before dark, an order came from the headquarters: SEND A GUARD TO 13 RUE, MCLEAN. They sent for me. First Sergeant said, Sergeant Barnett, get to me, go to Thirteen Rue, McLean, stand guard there tonight." With his little chickenshit grin, he wouldn't tell me the dangers that existed on this guard duty.

The captain said, "Barnett, take two men you can depend on. America has been in this city for thirty days. At this same spot where you will be, thirty men have been killed. No man has come out to tell what happened. They were all dead." I asked but nobody knew how they died. The captain said he didn't know. I walked away. I called my two seconds-in-command, Walter Bailey from Norfolk and Arthur Davis from Philly. Davis told Bailey that the first sergeant was trying to get Barnett killed, and he's going to get us killed. Bailey said, "Yep, that's right. I said they want a sergeant of the guard tonight. We are just three fellows trying to stay alive. Hand on the trigger, gun cocked, shoot, and ask questions later—those were my orders." I told the captain, "Tell the officer of the day don't come on Thirteen Rue McLean." God was with us; it was a very quiet night. The next morning at six thirty, we could hear our relief coming. We went in the building, and they called out three times. I saw them break rank with their weapons drawn, and we walked out. Those fellows really put a cursing on us. What they meant about the first sergeant was trying to get me killed. On Staten Island before we left, a young lady worked at the cafeteria that he liked, but she liked me. I liked her like a friend. I made the first move, and she said everything was OK. When she told me she was married and her husband was already overseas, something in me wouldn't let me touch that man's wife.

I would go to the cafeteria, and she would give me cartons of cigarettes for my men. I'm not going to name her. If she reads this book, she will know who I'm talking about. Thanks for all the candy and cigarettes you gave me. The first sergeant's name was Shattman. He disliked me because of her. One day, he asked her if he could come over to dinner during the weekend. She rapidly answered, "No, I'm having Corporal Barnett over." His brother and one of the sergeants laughed in his face. He put me on extra duty right then, and I didn't get a pass for the weekend. We were blessed that our neighbor company had pitched a tent in a French graveyard. They took some of the old wooden headstones and made a fire. Eisenhower started to court-martial the whole company. I told you we didn't stay there long. Two weeks after we left Roscoff, the hotel blew all to pieces. I still thank God for those two saved men. Soon we left there and moved close to the Belgian line, to an open field, where we pitched tents. It was not far from Paris, France. It was called Camp Twenty Grand. We had some stone hustlers in our company, some good gamblers and one pro dice shooter. He would bet you a $100 that he could throw four in two rolls. Some of us made pretty good money. My sergeant, a buck sarge (I was a technical sarge), made nearly three thousand dollars. He was sending the money to his wife. He said, "Barnett, I want to buy a house when I get out. We were living with my in-laws when I came to the army. One day, we had a mail call. Everybody was sitting around reading. I had twenty-one letters. You always read your wife's letter first. I saw him drop his head, looking straight ahead. I asked him if everything was OK. He didn't say a word; he just handed the letter to me. She was with child by another man. I had to take over his duties. All he did was just walk around with his head down. I thought he was going to lose his mind.

I did a little hustling, made a thousand or so dollars. I sent my wife a few hundred, the rest to my mother. I knew I would have some money when I returned. As I said before, we had some from every walk of life, some right out of Sing Sing prison. He was there for life but was given the chance to stay or go in the army—his name was Colliar. I say a "little dice" because we didn't have anything but some nickels and pennies. Colliar came along and said, "You poor bastard, I'm going to take those pennies." The game slowly increased. Sergeant Edwards shot him out five thousand dollars. He got hot. He carried a switchblade razor in his pocket; and when he got mad with someone, he would brag, "I killed one SOB. I don't mind going back to prison. We made it very clear to him, "If you hurt someone in this company, you won't have a chance to go back to prison, we'll hang you right here." That cooled him down.

At Twenty Grand, I was in charge of a staging area for the new troops on their way to the front line. I was to show them their area, where they got their briefing about what was going on, what to expect. I went to meet the ship, a fresh new group right from the States. One of the first fellows I saw was the captain that we got rid of in Staten Island. I saluted him, and he returned the same. I briefed him on a few things. There were about ten thousand on that ship. While we were talking, I looked out the corner of my eye, and you will never guess who I saw coming off that ship—the WAC battalion from New York. Those same pretty young ladies had caught up with us. I sent word back to the company: the WACs are here. The boys dropped everything and came running. You talking about hugging and kissing. The lieutenant was calling attention, but those fellows weren't thinking about attention. Next I saw one of the boys hugging his girlfriend. You never know how much you miss a black woman until you look and see every kind of women but her. When you see her, you feel like Adam: this is bone of my bone, flesh of my flesh. That night we threw a party for them. For some dirty reason the next morning, we received orders to ship out.

Our destination was the South Pacific. We were the first group to leave Europe. Some of the fellows thought we were coming home. We caught a freight train, a boxcar full of hay to lie on. It took us about four days to reach southern France. Marsa was a large port, and it took us about a week to get processed. Those fellows sold those winter uniforms. It was warm there, and they issued summer uniforms, but I kept mine. The French had plenty of money. They would buy anything you had to sell except peanut butter. They said peanut butter would choke the baby. By that time, news had reached us that Hitler had surrendered, but the Japanese hadn't. We boarded USS *Wagner*, a new troop ship right out the state. That was some ship. Seven thousand black and one hundred white GIs—for forty-five days we sailed. Out on the coast of Morocco, the water was blue, the sand was white. It was a sight to see. I watched dry land as long as I could, and soon it faded out of sight. The sun and moon looked like it rose and set in the ocean. From the front to the rear of that large ship, there was a dice game or card game. We had just got paid off. Those GIs had plenty of money. Three fellows I know won over $5,000. Spicer, the expert dice man, won six thousand.

Soon we got to Panama. We stayed there for two days because the ship had lost one of its propellers. We went through the Panama Canal, and that was a sight to see. The Pacific Ocean is smooth sailing, not like the Atlantic, which is rocky. You ate twice a day. When your unit went through, you had to go through with them, or you didn't eat. Some of the fellows in the dice game who had a hot hand or winning at cards would miss chow. That's why the sailors would come in and say, "You missed chow." You're hungry now, pocket full of money, or your belly growling and you've lost it all. A sailor would come by with a hot loaf, right out of the galley, a stick of butter, and a quart of milk. You would say, "Hey, sailor, what you want for that?" The sailor would ask $40, for a 15-cent loaf of bread, a quart of milk costing no more than 25 cents, and 5-cent butter. He knew you're hungry and you'd pay. Those sailors cashed in on the other soldiers' big time. But when they came ashore looking for women, the GIs had all the cat houses, so the sailors had to pay a big price—cat and mouse. Now there were three sissies on the boat. They beat them up so bad; they liked to kill them. The captain had to lock them up till we got to Manila. Two were in our company, and I won't give their names. Soon after forty-eight days, we arrived.

I want to tell you something I did on the ship. I got on galley detail. Every five o'clock in the morning, I would report to the galley. I would go to the cold storage to get food for the galley, so I ate first. When the detail was over, I had a big coat, and I looked like three fellows with fruits. I sold apples a $1, oranges $1, and bananas $1. After forty-eight days, I had a pretty good piece of change in my pocket. I shot a little dice and threw two snake eyes for $400. For those who don't know what snake eyes means, you lost. I could go to these fifteen to twenty, but I would break those fellows. I would go up to the big boys, where they were shooting one hundred to two hundred and lose. The boys would see me coming and say, "Here comes Barnett, let him in." Now we were going ashore. The black GIs were glad to see us. They were outnumbered five to one. The whites had downtown Manila. The black GIs couldn't go downtown. They had spent the army money to fix up downtown. The black GIs had to stay in the Walled City. This is where the Japanese put up a ferocious battle. There still were some skulls and human parts when we arrived.

There was a river that divided the city. Black GIs couldn't go across the bridge. If you did, they would get some of your hind part. MacArthur's headquarters was only three hundred yards from where all this was going on. The same day we arrived, I had to get a group of men to rope off the area where we camped. The people were around us by the thousands. Some where stealing the GIs' belongings, so I had to get six men to guard the place. The captain gave the first order. He said, "Barnett, please don't lay your hand on any of them. If you do, MacArthur will court-martial all of us, we will never go home." We pitched our pup tents. That same night it rained one of those monsoon rains. The pup tents fell down, and those guys got wringing wet. I had to pull guard duty all night by myself. I said something to one GI, and he cursed me out. I didn't bother another one. When you came into a new area, you were restricted for twenty-four hours. Two GIs came to me. One said, "I know we are restricted, but I've been out on that beat for forty-eight hours, and I haven't seen any women."

I said, "Why don't you wait till twenty-four hours are up before you go cross town."

"Those GIs told us how they are here, all you have to do is not tell anybody."

I turned my back and said, "I don't see you."

They said, "Thank you, Sarge. I always thought you were a fine fellow."

They went downtown, right where the fellows told us about. They went in one of the fine spots, sat down with ribbons and three battle stars. The custom in the Philippines was when the ladies served you and they weren't too busy, they would come to the table and sit down with you.

One of those pretty young ladies came to the table and sat down. She could tell you just came in. She asked them to tell her something about Europe and what these medals meant. A white GI came over, sat down, and started talking. He had been drinking, and all at once, he started crying. "I used to be in France and a damn nigger soldier shot me," he said. "I liked to have lost my life. I swore I would get even with one of those black bastards." He started pulling out an army .45 pistol. Williams said he caught him before he got it out, hit him between the eyes, and he fell backward. All hell broke loose. They would have killed those fellows, but the waitress slipped them out the back door. I forget the one who said he didn't know he could run so fast. They came back to the company and told what happened. They woke up the old Alabama sergeant Harris. They got three truckloads and went down to the far end of town. They started kicking hind parts all the way to the end. They had those white boys jumping out the window. I was the sergeant of the guards. I was supposed to know everything that happened when it happened. Early the next morning, our hind parts were standing at attention open ranks. MacArthur and his whole staff were there. I was the only man they questioned. The captain said, "Barnett, did any of these men from this company leave this area last night?" I said, "No, sir." The captain said, "Are you sure?" Right before MacArthur and his staff, I said, "Yes, sir." Standing there like a statue, MacArthur said, "Carry on, soldier," and they left. The captain looked at me after they left, and, right before the company, said, "Captain, you have just seen the most convincing liar in the country." The sergeant said, "Barnett, I thank you. We would have been shipped right out to the front line." He knew who those fellows were, but he never mentioned it anymore.

The first sergeant came by with his chickenshit grin and said, "You just saved your hind parts and ours." I knew he didn't like me. Every chance he got, if he had a dirty job, he would give it to me and my men. But they stuck by me. They knew what was happening. To Sergeant Shattman, I hope you are still alive to read this. If not, I hope your kids will read it. You had a fine brother. The people were hungry, and they ate the food we threw away in the garbage can. He gave me the job of driving them away. That was the second time that I cried in the army. The first was when almost all my neighbor company got blown up. "Me," I said, "I can't drive these people away. Can't you see they're starving?" Shattman said, "You'll do it or I'll bust you back down to private." If I had known I was coming home in the next six months, I would have told him to take them and stick them. I couldn't feed all of them. There was one family I helped. When I finished eating, I would go back through the line, fill my helmet full, and give it to her. In return, she would wash my work uniform. I enrolled in the Philippine Institute. I went there for six months to brush up on my math.

We had quite a few college young men. Sometimes we would get out our pencil and paper to see who knew the most. They didn't know that I hadn't finished high school. I stayed close to a math teacher, and he taught me a lot. He taught math at Virginia Union. His name was Buck, short for Buckert. He said, "If you learned the formula, you could work most math problems." I must admit I didn't learn a whole lot, what with all those pretty young ladies smiling at you, saying, "Hello, Joe!" One fellow asked me, "Aren't you going to try to learn their language?" I said, "Yes, how much?" That was all I wanted to know. Soon my orders came down. "Sergeant Barnett, you can go home." I was the first one in the company. They went by points, and I had fifty-seven points. There were other GIs that had the same amount of points, but AB ordered that I was the first to leave.

When I got on the ship, it began to sink in, *You're leaving your company behind.* I wished we could have come home together like we left, but it wasn't meant to be. We had been living together for three years like brothers because we had to depend on each other. I stood at the rear of the ship. I watched Manila until it faded out of sight. Soon I felt a few tears rolling down my face. I knew I would never see these fellows again. So I turned around and went down below to face a new company of GIs. I didn't know a soul.

But I soon started asking if there were anybody from Louisiana. The ship was loaded, going to Texas, Mississippi. I was coming home to a young lady I knew very little about, a son two and a half years old that I had never seen, a mother, a father, and a host of brothers and sisters. Most of all, I was coming home to the woman who adopted me from when I was one year old, Ollie Riggs, my mother who taught me how to be a man and, most of all, about God. But I still shed a few tears when I left my comrades. Something I saw on my way home—we were to have 1,200 men, and now we had 1,000. When the ship would turn over to the merchant marines, to keep from taking inventory of the merchandise, they would throw it overboard. For four days I had detail throwing food overboard. When I arrived in the States, people had food stamps, and I was surprised. The trip was twenty-eight days. I met an older fellow named Kooncan. He lived very close to my hometown, and we got into a card game. The stakes were pretty good. I knew I was a little better than he was, so I drew him five games. Every game he would put down $25 or more. When I got him where I wanted, I dealt him a pat hand. All he needed was one card. But I dealt myself one. All I needed was one card also. He picked up his cards. I could see he was happy, so I said, "I see I can't beat you, it's getting close to chow time, let's go double or nothing, winner take all."

He liked to break his hand getting in his pocket. I had never picked up my hand. We did an extra $20. So as soon as I picked up my hand, I said, "You have something I don't. I'd like to call this bet off." He said, "You nigger, you said winner take all, so you can't back down." I asked him to put up another $20, and he did, so I said OK. I knew the first card was mine, and the second was his. He flipped the card and dropped it. To his surprise, I laid my hand down—a pat hand. I can't describe the reaction on his face. He called me everything in the book. It didn't help him any. I had almost all the money he was to take his wife and kids. I laid down that night not far from the old man. I could hear him mumbling something all night. After chow the next morning, I called him and gave him every dime he had lost. My conscience wouldn't let me take the old fellow's money that he had for his family although he lost it legally, or did I cheat the older fellow?

When we arrived in San Francisco, there was a big greeting party with music. I was the first man down the walk. I heard a few voices call out, "Hello, Sergeant Barnett!" I said to myself, *Could this be some of the boys and girls I grew up with?* No, it wasn't. It was the beautiful WAC company we left in Europe. Now they're here again. You talk about some old-time kissing. They were concerned about the other fellows. I told them they were OK. They gave a party for us the next night, and the following morning, the post commander asked us not to go AWOL because he was going to get us processed as soon as possible so we could be on our way home. I tried to call my sister in Los Angeles, but I made a mistake in her number. There was a line of fellows behind me trying to call home. After three days, we were on our way to Camp Fannin, Texas. The train stopped in Bakersfield, California, to pick up some supplies, and while we were doing that, the captain in charge thought he would give us a little treat on Uncle Sam. We went in this cafeteria, and the owner said he could serve the white boys, but not these niggers. The captain said, "Then you won't serve any of us," and we walked out.

Some of the fellows felt a little bad about what happened. It didn't bother me at all because I was on my way home to a little town where I could be served anywhere. Some of them had risked their lives away from their families for two to three years, came back home, and couldn't buy a sandwich from a white restaurant. I enjoyed myself on the train with clean beads and white sheets, plus I was on my way home where people knew me from birth. What more could you ask for? After two or three days, we arrived in Texas. They told us, "I know you fellows are in a hurry to get home, and we're going to help you to go." Two days later on Saturday morning, they gave me $50 on top of the money I already had. I would've had $1,000 if I had kept the money I won from that older fellow. That was my second time giving money back. On our trip to Manila, Colliar had $600 in a money belt. He had been up all night gambling. He was dead asleep and his shirt was wide open with the belt almost about to fall off him. I took it. I didn't want some of those other fellows "who would steal the sweet out of a cookie." That's what the old folks would say if you were a thief. When he woke up his money was gone. I kept it until I came back from chow. I could see the worry on his face. I handed him his money. He thanked me, and that was enough for me.

Saturday by noon, about nine of us were headed to Louisiana. We caught a taxi from Camp Fannie to Shreveport! I was trying to catch the train; the train would get me there that night. That was my plan, but when we got to Shreveport, the train was gone. I wanted to catch all the farmers, black and white, sitting around Delta Drug Store, sipping on booze, talking about their farms and the war. Instead, I caught the bus, and it looked like it stopped at every other house. I arrived at two thirty that morning. I can't tell you how happy I was. I had more money in my pocket than some farmers made in a year. Besides, I had sent $1,000 to my mother, which I knew would be there when I arrived. So many fellows had sent money and the parents had spent it. I went to Sam Scurr Saloon, the only place I found open. I went to the rear of the place, where all the big shots would gamble. They played skin. I heard some had lost two to three bales of cotton. A black lady ran the game. I walked in the back, and she jumped up from the table, hugged me, and said, "I know Ollie is going to be some kind of happy when she sees her handsome son come home." When I came out, before I left home, I met a young lady who would always ask me for money to get her a drink. She hadn't changed. I knew she wasn't really all there, but I treated her just like I did all the other young ladies. She asked me, "Where are you going?" I told her I was heading to my godmother's house, who was her aunt. She said, "Don't walk down that dark street by yourself. Things have changed since you left here. A couple of fellows came home, you see those four fellows sitting over there, they were a part of it. I'll call you a cab." So I took her advice. Joe Knight was the taxi driver, an old friend. We both lived in Trinidad. He was much older. He was the one who shamed me when I was trying to learn to smoke. He said, "Look at him, he's going to kill himself before he gets grown." I threw all my tobacco away.

I arrived at my godmother's house and knocked on the door. My godmother said, "Who is it?" I said, "Pudding." She said, "Who?" I said, "Pudding!" I heard her jump out of bed. "Thank God! My godson's back home." She opened the door and jumped around my neck, hugging and kissing me. I guess she weighed 125 pounds. That's why everybody called her Little Girl. We talked almost till day. I got in the bed right behind her. The next morning, she had to go to work. She was cooking for my former boss. I was still in bed, and soon the door opened and one of the prettiest young ladies walked in. "Hello, Pudding!" she said. I said hello back but with surprise. She knew me or heard my godmother call my name. She said, "I know you, but you don't remember me."

"How could I not remember you if I ever knew you?" I said.

"My name is Deatsy Cook. I live on the Sevare plantation."

"You did? I thought I knew all the families around there."

She said, "My last name wasn't Cook."

"OK."

She said, "I used to see you and Samelka. I was a little smaller, that's why you didn't pay me any attention. I was a poor little girl. The Phillips were the big shots."

I said, "Don't get me mixed up. I have never failed to recognize a person due to his statue or condition."

She said, "Now that we know each other, you live here and I live in the next room."

I knew right then that meant trouble for me. She was good-looking and classy, everything a man could wish for. Only thing, she was married and so was I. Her husband was in DC working, and my wife was in Norfolk, Virginia. I will stop right here.

The next day, I met that schoolteacher I told you about earlier. She was doing a little showcase shopping. I walked up behind her and touched her on the shoulder. She turned around, threw up both hands, ran to me, and threw her arms around my neck, hugging me. She said, "I'm so glad you're back home." And I'm saying to myself, *I'm so glad I'm a man now.* The teacher said, "I'm not afraid anymore."

My sister from Chicago had come home. We met and caught a taxi to the country. When I got out of that taxi, Trinidad had never looked so pretty. This is where the farmers came together and talked about their farms or whatever. They called it Cross Roads. I looked to my left and saw a familiar face about a hundred yards away feeding his horses. I called out to him one of those long hellos. "Hellooo, Mr. Rabbit." He knew my voice and called back, "Hellooo, Mr. Fox."

That was my uncle, Steve Kincy. I could hear him call my Aunt Ida. "What is it, Steve?" she asked. "Mr. Fox is home!" he answered. Soon I saw the door open. She came out to meet me, half trotting, wiping water from her eyes. She said, "Thank you, God, for bringing my sister's son back home safe." We hugged and kissed right in the middle of the highway. My voice went across that plantation. It looked like the wind carried my voice all across the farm. The farmer stopped his mule in the middle of the field, and he came. You would never guess who else was coming, half running and half walking! Remember the gal I told you about from the plum orchard, Dina Riggs? She ain't cursing me. Now she's thanking God he brought me back safe. We hugged and kissed. We laughed. "Oh boy," she said, "you sure look good in that suit." Soon I heard another voice. "Ollieeee! Ollieeee! Ollie Ho!" That was Hattie—Hattie Riggs, my Uncle Pete's wife. She continued, "Pudding's home, your son's home." Ollie and Uncle Bus were working in the garden. She dropped everything. I could see her running about ten yards, then walking and clapping her hands. Bus was right behind her. When I saw her clapping her hands together, she was quite a distance. I knew she was saying, "Thank you, God, for bringing my son back home." I had been gone close to five years. I took off running toward her, and soon we embraced each other. I can't put it into words or express on paper how I felt. Soon Uncle Bus joined us. I hadn't seen him in over twelve years. My sister Beatrice Washington, Mother, Uncle Bus, and I went on down that old dusty road I have traveled from one year old. Many dark nights it was so dark you couldn't see your hand in front of your face. Now it looked like Wall Street in New York City.

Soon we arrived at the old farmhouse. Nothing had changed. I went in the guest room. That was my room after I turned fifteen. Mother said, "Son, you need your own room." The older fellow slept in the room next to me. The brass bed was shining as usual, the "shiftrow" with some of my clothing still hanging in place. I looked around. I was just happy to be back home. Mother fixed dinner for my sister and me. I always knew she was a good cook, but that meal looked like she put her heart and soul into it. Or maybe it was just me. The news got out that Pudding was home, and every night for three weeks we got together. What a time we had. Some had been to war like I did. Some did not, but it didn't matter. We still had a lot to talk about. One Saturday night Mother came to town and said, "Son, it's time to come home." I said OK. Around one o'clock, we went out in the country. Somebody wrote Kizzie and told her I was home. This was the young lady that I mentioned before, that after spending five minutes with her, you forgot everything she did. She arrived from LA and came to the house. The next morning, we were making plans. I was going back to LA with her.

For some reason God sent my mother in the next room for something. She overheard my plans. A few hours later she called me aside. She said, "Son, you're grown now and I can't tell you what to do or not to do, but if you leave your wife and child and go back with this girl, God ain't going to bless you." These are just the words she said, and they hit me like a ton of bricks. For a few minutes I didn't know what to say. I had to tell Kizzie that I couldn't go back to LA with her. She cried and so did I. But I couldn't go against God or he wouldn't bless me. I went back to Shreveport with her and spent the night. The next morning, I caught the train back home. Mother said, "Son, you had a chance to marry that girl. I think she would have made you a good wife. I love her, but you have a wife and child in Virginia. Send for your wife and child so I can see them both." But Mother added, "Son, she ain't coming, I have that feeling."

I wrote the letter for her and the boy to come. "I was home, and my family want to see you and my son."

The very next week I received a letter back: "I can't come, your son is sick."

Mother said, "I didn't think she was coming, that boy is not sick. Go home, your wife and son need you. I'm not trying to run you away from home. This is your home as long as Bus and I live."

The very next night, I caught the train down in my army uniform. Thursday morning at eight thirty, I knocked on the door.

"Who is it?"

I said, "Barnett."

I heard her coming downstairs. She opened the door and said, "Hi, you're back." No hug, no kiss, so I said, "Ya'll I'm back, hell had jumped in me already. I've been gone three years and no hug, no kiss."

I didn't smile one time, and soon I asked, "Where is my son?" She said, "He's upstairs." I went upstairs and saw a handsome little two-and-a-half-year-old boy. He looked straight at me. She said, "Butch, this is your father." I spoke and said, "Hi, young man." He answered back hi. I knew right then that whatever the devil was saying to me, he might as well shut up. I wasn't going anywhere and leave my son. For a week, everywhere I went, he was right behind me, looking me over. I said to myself, *What's this boy thinking?* One thing came to my mind. *He's thinking, you don't look like the fellows that came here while you were gone.* She was living with her sister when I met her. Two months after we got married, I was gone. Later that evening, her sister came in. She ran to me, hugged me, and said, "Barnett, I'm so glad you're home." For a while, I thought I had married the wrong sister.

The next morning, I got up early and went to my old job. Everybody was happy to see me. My supervisor asked me if I wanted to take a few weeks off. I said, "No, I have a wife and son to feed." He said, "OK, Monday morning, I'll see you." He shook my hand and said, "I sure am glad to have you back."

Monday morning, bright and early, I walked in the office. I thought I was going to go back with my old gang. They sent me to a new department—sanitation. I took one look at that job and walked away. I heard someone coming behind me. "Young fellow," he said, "look around." He was a World War I vet, ex-sergeant. He caught me by the hand and said, "Come on back. It's a dirty job, but the war is over and they're going to start laying off. This job will be the last one they hit." He asked if I was married and I said, "Yes, sir, with one son." He said, "So you're going to need to work, come on back." He caught me by the hand, and I went on back. I had on clean shined shoes, and my pants were creased. The fellows gave me a pair of pants, shirt, and shoes, and off I went. I caught on real quick. The old man's name was Gill, and he always seemed to like me. After a day or two, I met the fellows. The job didn't seem so dirty after all. We had a shower where we could bathe in the evening. After a week, a fellow named Mayson, who carried a gang, had been watching me work. He asked the quart man he could have me to work with him. The quartman gave the OK. The two of us went to another incinerator that hung outside the base. I had taken up a trade in the army as crane operator, but that was a white man's job. I could do more with that crane than they could. I was trained to operate it blindfolded. You had to operate sometimes at night, and you couldn't have a light. You had to work by a bell from your signal man. If you're out there with a light, an airplane could come and drop a bomb on you because of that light.

It took me thirty years before I could get a chance to operate. I wouldn't take it. A few fellows did. I had a good warm and a comfortable job. I wasn't going to sit out on those piers in the wintertime, icicles hanging off the crane as big as your arm. You were lifting bombs and torpedoes onto ships and subs. One slip and you could kill a lot of people, including yourself. Back to the incinerator, Mayson liked to get himself killed and me with him. Thursday was payday, and he got in his car at twelve o'clock, not far from the job. A fellow ran a liquor house, and Mayson was going with the man's wife. Someone had told the man every Thursday, he would come and see his wife. His name was Joe Mayson, but whoever spoke to him just said Mayson. The husband called him Joe. We were sitting at his table eating dinner. She would fix dinner for us every Thursday. Sometimes the fellow would come while we were there. He'd say, "Hello, Joe! You're welcome here, you are one of my best customers." When we left, Mayson would drop five or six dollars on the table and get himself a drink as we go. This Thursday, our luck almost ran out. We were sitting at the table eating when her husband walked in with his gun in his hand. His wife asked, "What are you doing home with that gun in your hand?" He said, "Somebody told me that damn nigger named Mayson was going with you, come here every Thursday. I came back home to kill the SOB." He said, "Joe, you are OK with me, you and your young friend. If he had noticed me, he would have known something was wrong." I got choked at the table. On my way to the car, I was hoping he wouldn't find out who we were. Mayson thought quickly. All at once, he had to go to the bank to cash his check. I really gave him a cursing out. "You like to get me and yourself killed." Later we laughed about it. Every evening I came home, I felt like I was coming home to a young lady who had a son I loved, and they depended on me. I wasn't satisfied living like that. I wanted to feel like I was coming home to my wife and kid.

One night, I got on my knees and prayed about the way I thought. The reception I received after three years was still with me. Soon I had a beautiful daughter to come. Everything changed. I couldn't get home fast enough to see my handsome son and beautiful daughter. Soon I had another son who was sickly. I thought I was going to lose him. I cried out to the Lord not to take my son, and he heard me. A few years later, another son came. I thought he was the nicest little fellow. Through the years, I look back over my life and realize how blessed I was to meet a strange young lady, who didn't smoke or drink. Not a street woman, just satisfied to stay home to take care of our kids. For seventeen years, she stayed home to take care of our most valuable possessions, our kids. I have to admit she did a very good job. I did everything I could do to keep her happy, so I could go. All she had to do was say, and I said here it is. I kept my family well dressed, had plenty of food on the table, and had a decent roof over their heads. If anybody did without, let it be me. I would tell my wife that if a stranger comes to my home hungry and there are two slices of bread, give one to the stranger and she take the other, let me do without. I have always, from my childhood until now, had food on my table more than I could consume. I was over seventy-five before I ever spent a night in a hospital. In 1980, I was diagnosed with prostate cancer. When the doctor told me, I cried like a two year old. I couldn't help it.

I went home and sat in my car for a while. I didn't want my wife to see me cry. I walked in the house and didn't look at her. She asked me, "What did the doctor say?" And I said, "I have cancer." She said, "Well, don't you claim it." I went in the bedroom, closed the door, bowed down before the Almighty, and wept and prayed. She asked, "Don't you want to call the family to come and pray for you?" I said, "No, this is a battle I have to fight alone." That night I took a good hot bath, dried off, and went back to the same place I bowed before—the foot of my bed. Only this time, I was just like I came in the world. I prayed and asked the Lord not to let me die from cancer and not to let me worry about it.

The next day, I went to fasting and praying. Well, I'm still here. Fifteen years later, my doctor told me it was spreading. God had showed me in my sleep before I went through my operation. When I came out half an hour later, my wife and oldest son were there. The first thing they said was the doctor couldn't find a thing. I told them, "I knew that all the time."

After my father passed away, God was good to him. He wasn't a saved man. He didn't go to church. He knew God's word, and he would always read the Bible. Mother used to always say, "You are reading your salvation," but he demonstrated or lived a Christian life better than some Christians. God loved him, so he told him to get his house in order because he was going to die. So he called all his children, and we came with our families. We talked about him behind his back. We said he was just scared because he had never been real sick. He got saved. When I walked into the hospital, the first thing he said to me was, "Boy, I've excepted Jesus as my Lord and Savior." Six months later, I got a call that he had passed away. Mother lived about four years more. She passed away. Bus was gone, and in 1979, Ollie Riggs was found lying on the floor.

I stayed and took care of her for almost six months until the doctor sent me home. The doctor said, "If you don't go, they will bury you instead of your mother." When I had gotten to where she lived, I couldn't sleep anymore. It was 105 degrees every day I was there. My mother couldn't stand for a fan to blow on her or the house. I was on the verge of a nervous breakdown. I prayed constantly for help, and my prayers were answered. I couldn't stay away, but a week and a half, I got a call; her natural son didn't want to put his hands on her. His granddaughter called me, so I returned. I had to make a tough decision to put her in a nursing home. The family, the church family, the judge of the town all told me it was the right decision. I just couldn't see it right; it looked like I was throwing her away or turning my back on her when she needed me the most.

Soon they got to me, and I took her there. It was a nice place, if a nursing home can be a nice place. When I walked out the door, I waited a few minutes and opened it again. She was still looking at the door, and she waved good-bye to me. I knew I wouldn't ever see her alive again. Tears came rolling down my face. I couldn't hold them back. I had a Ryder truck with some of her things. I had another fellow with me, and while he drove, I cried halfway across Mississippi.

Now everybody's dead. Oh, my Aunt Lake had passed away. She was a loving aunt, and she loved her sister's children. When we went to her home, she always met us at the gate with open arms. There was no more place. My wife and her family started having a reunion every fourth of July. One day, she said, "My kids will grow up not knowing the kin folks on your side. I'm going to send them an invitation." I said, "They aren't coming." She said, "We won't know if we don't try." Then I agreed and sent them. The first group was my sister Virginia and her kids, friends, and in-laws. For a week, we had ourselves some fun. They didn't think I knew, but they questioned, "How would we treat them?" I treated them like I treated the others who came because they are my sisters and brothers and families. I am a family man.

Because they told them how much fun they had, this started our family reunions. This past summer in 2004, they met in Vicksburg, Mississippi. Next year, 2005, they're having it in Norfolk, Virginia, at the first week of June. Come and join us. You won't forget the Barnetts and the Stewarts. I hope the Riggs will come in and the Ransons who make up half of our family. Ollie Riggs always told me, "Son, Jim and Shug are your natural parents. I adopted you at one year old, but they couldn't love you anymore than I do!" She demonstrated it. I don't know what God promised Dathney or what Dathney asked God, but he really blessed her blood across America. Even my family is growing. Two beautiful daughters, three handsome sons—they all found mates. They did almost as good as I did. I have thirteen grandchildren, and I've lost count of the great-grandchildren that I have.

Out of all my training coming up, some I ignored until it caught up with me. There were some that stuck with me that I didn't disregard.

1. *Son, don't abuse your wife and children. If you do, you will live to regret it.*

2. *Extend the hand of courtesy to the other man first. If he or she is any kind of person at all, they will extend the same courtesy back to you. If he or she doesn't, move on; they aren't worth dealing with.*

And to my brothers and sisters or whatever relation I am to you, may God richly bless you in your going out and coming in, in your laughter and in your tears, in your ups and downs. When that day comes when we all stand before God, he will wipe all your tears. May God bless the readers.

This is the end of *The Little Pine Tree That Escaped the Ax*
by Arthur Barnett Sr.
better known across the country as Uncle Pudding

PS: Shortly after I finished this story, the very first Sunday at 6:30 a.m., I was rushed to the hospital. A few hours later, I was ready to come home, but they kept me. I believe I made a great mistake. I let them persuade me to let them put a pacemaker in my heart. They almost paralyzed my left arm. I was in the hospital for two weeks and couldn't walk.

I am home now, trying to recover slowly but surely. God has sent me help that I didn't know was available. My kids stood by their mother while I was away. Now I'm running on my left leg and right arm, but I'm thankful for the two. I can't complain. I saw a man that didn't have any. The leg is getting better. The gout has me in the right foot. I will kick that too! Good evening, everybody!